*How the "Prospective Bride and Groom" Match Up... According to the Supposed Groom:*

Marriage? A wife is my crafty little brothers' crazy notion, not mine. After all, I've got a ranch to run, three orphaned kids to raise. I don't have time for wedding plans. Plus, Calley doesn't know the first thing about ranching life. She can't even mount a horse without scaring the cows. And she'd have to be "mommy" to three precocious boys. So, the only vows I'm going to make are to my brothers.

"That's what *he* thinks!"
—Christopher, Timothy and Wynne Slade

*Dear Reader,*

Imagine: You're a single woman who works in the Men's Suits department of a store. You sell suit after suit to hunk after hunk. They ask how they look, they ask about alterations—but they never ask you out. So, you slip a little note about yourself in the pocket of your favorite suit—then wait for the man of your dreams to buy it.

He buys the suit. He finds the note. But it's not the note you wrote! And that's how Clare Banning of Carolyn Zane's *Single in Seattle* eventually finds herself measuring that very man for a tuxedo....

In Carla Neggers's *The Groom Who (Almost) Got Away*, Calley Hastings practically had Max Slade all measured for a tux, too. But then he just up and left her without a word. Now, she finally finds out why when his three little orphaned brothers hoodwink her into coming to their Wyoming ranch....

Next month, you'll find two new Yours Truly novels by Lass Small and Celeste Hamilton—with a new (but probably very familiar!) name at the bottom of the Dear Reader letter. I'm taking over the reins of Silhouette Romance, and Leslie Wainger, senior editor of Intimate Moments, will now also be bringing you two terrific Yours Truly titles every month. I hope you've enjoyed the books so far—and hope you'll enjoy all the wonderful ones to come.

Yours truly,

*Melissa Senate*

Melissa Senate
Senior Editor

---

Please address questions and book requests to:
Silhouette Reader Service
U.S.: 3010 Walden Ave., P.O. Box 1325, Buffalo, NY 14269
Canadian: P.O. Box 609, Fort Erie, Ont. L2A 5X3

# CARLA NEGGERS

## The Groom Who (Almost) Got Away

SILHOUETTE YOURS TRULY™

Published by Silhouette Books

America's Publisher of Contemporary Romance

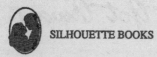

SILHOUETTE BOOKS

ISBN 0-373-52022-0

THE GROOM WHO (ALMOST) GOT AWAY

## About the author

**CARLA NEGGERS** finished writing her first book and mailed it off to an agent four months after her first child was born, when she was twenty-four years old and so broke she had to rent a typewriter. The agent took her on, the book sold, and since then she's become known for her wit, humor and fast-paced stories, which appear regularly on romance bestseller lists and have been translated into more than two dozen languages. *Publishers Weekly* has called her work "engaging" and "highly entertaining," and *Affaire de Coeur* has said, "One is never disappointed reading anything by Carla Neggers." She has received the *Romantic Times* Reviewer's Choice Award four times, and last year had a story in an anthology that hit both the *New York Times* and *USA Today* bestseller lists.

A magna cum laude graduate of Boston University, Carla gives writing workshops all over the country and serves as a volunteer for the Authors Guild Committee on Free Expression. She and her husband, a native Tennessean, live in Vermont with their two children, their aging golden retriever…and, if her son gets his way, a lizard.

**To Joan Johnston**

# *Prologue*

——————— ◆ ———————

Christopher Slade was eleven years old and convinced no one understood him. No one would care if he died. No one believed he had any feelings at all.

He ducked into one of the storage rooms in the old stone stable his grandfather had built decades ago. It wasn't used for much of anything anymore. Christopher quietly shut the door behind him. His little brothers wouldn't miss him. Jimmy wouldn't notice he was gone until he didn't show up for supper. Even Max wouldn't notice.

He could rot out in the stable before anybody noticed he wasn't around.

Big, fat tears rolled down his cheeks as he sat on the cold floor and leaned against a huge old trunk, his bony knees tucked up under his chin. He would never be as strong as Max, he thought. He'd never seen his older brother cry. Oh, Max had said it was okay for Christopher and his little brothers to cry; crying didn't make anybody weak. But Christopher had never seen Max shed a tear.

He squeezed his eyes shut, but still the tears came.

Four years ago today, Christopher thought. Four years and nobody but him remembered. He'd just been seven. A little kid. He'd hardly known what was happening.

A sob escaped despite his best efforts to keep his mouth clamped shut.

He missed his mom and dad. Max said that was normal; of course he would miss them. It was a sign, Max said, of how much they'd all meant to each other. He'd also said that Christopher shouldn't worry so much about getting over the loss of his parents, but of going on with his own life knowing that their loss was a part of who he was. Christopher thought he understood. And most of the time he got along just fine and laughed and messed around and just lived his life on Black Creek Ranch. But not always. Sometimes he just started thinking about his parents and couldn't stop.

His mom had had white blond hair and green eyes, and he could remember every detail of her smile and the way she would ruffle his hair and tell him not to worry so much. He was her cowboy poet, she would say. And his dad, lots older than his mom, had always said nothing in his life, nothing was more important than his boys—meaning the three young ones, not Max. Never meaning Max. Even at seven, Christopher had known that. In a way, Max wasn't like his father's son at all.

They'd died four years ago today, his mom and dad. Max had left New York and come home to Wyoming to take care of his three little half brothers and tend the family ranch. They'd done all right together, Max and Christopher and Timothy and Wynne, with Jimmy there to keep up the house and grumble and make sure the boys had baths. But Christopher wished he could see his parents again, even for just five minutes to tell them goodbye—to hear them say he would be all right without them. He wrote poems about them. He hadn't shown them to anyone, not even Max.

He brushed away his tears, feeling better just for thinking about his parents and the night they'd died. Wynne was only six and hardly remembered them. Timothy was nine and didn't like talking about them. Sometimes Christopher just didn't know what to say or think or anything, because nobody understood how he felt, and he couldn't explain even if he'd wanted to.

Getting to his feet, he pulled the string that dangled from the naked light bulb, which was screwed into a socket on the low ceiling, casting the small, crowded room into shadows and dim light. He seldom came in here, just when he and Timothy and Wynne were playing hide-and-seek. One whole wall was shelves, lined with old books and bundles of papers, iron boxes and junk from the ranch, some rotting hats, a pair of spurs. There were a couple of old wooden chairs and a rolltop desk shoved up against another wall, and just the one trunk.

Maybe there was treasure in it, Christopher thought. Gold, silver, secrets. He remembered how his mom used to send him out on scavenger hunts.

The top of the trunk was wooden and flat, functional, a little soft with age, nothing at all like the ornate, antique trunk his mother had bought for the study at the house. It creaked when he raised the lid.

Inside, however, was no treasure, not that he'd really expected any. He'd just wanted to do something to help him stop thinking.

Christopher squinted in the dim light, making out textbooks on finance and economics, the annual report of some company with a picture of New York City on the front and a couple of photo albums. A thin one with a burgundy cover was on top. Christopher flipped it open without taking it from the trunk.

Pictures of Max. A whole page of them. Pictures Christopher had never seen before.

Intrigued, he dragged the album out and laid it on the desk in the best light. In one picture, Max and a dark-haired woman in glasses were standing on an enormous set of stairs in front of a huge, columned building definitely not located in Wyoming.

Christopher had never seen the dark-haired woman before. She was smiling. He thought she was kind of pretty.

And Max was smiling in a way Christopher couldn't remember seeing him smile. Not since he'd come back to Wyoming, anyway. He looked carefree. Happy. As if he couldn't imagine being happier.

Obviously, Christopher thought, the picture had been taken before his parents' accident.

He turned the page. There were more pictures of his older brother and the dark-haired woman, but Christopher's attention was drawn to a couple of folded sheets of white paper tucked between the pages of the photo album. He opened them up carefully, his heart pounding. Max would have his hide for snooping.

The top page was dated four years ago to the day.

Dear Calley,
I don't know where to begin, or how...

The next words were smudged, the paper mottled, as if it had been wet and then dried. Christopher turned to the next page. Same date, same uneven handwriting.

Dear Calley,
I'll get right to the point. My father and his wife were killed today in a car accident in Wyoming. They have three little boys, my brothers, who need me. I have to go home to them. They have no one else. I'm too confused myself, and I know you, and I can't ask you to come home with me. It would be selfish, no matter how much I want you to be with me. I can't...

The letter ended there, midsentence. Some of the words were blurred. Whatever had spilled on the first letter must have spilled on this one, too, he thought.

Christopher could hear someone hollering for him. Max.

He quickly refolded the letters and put them back where he'd found them, shutting the photo album, then the lid to the trunk. He pulled the string on the light bulb and slipped out of the dark room into the cool, crisp air of the Wyoming spring.

"There you are," Max said, coming around the corner of the small stable.

He didn't look like the man in the pictures Christopher had just seen. This Max Slade looked so much older and harder, as if he would never be as happy as he'd been that day on the steps with the dark-haired woman. He didn't even wear the same clothes. In the picture, he'd had on a suit and tie. Now he wore dusty old jeans and scruffy boots and a flannel shirt with frayed elbows, not because he couldn't afford a new one, but because he didn't care. He would say this one still had life left in it. His hair, darker than that of his little half brothers because his mother had been part Sioux, was longer, messier, and his face had more lines in it, and his smile—well, it wasn't at all like his smile in the picture.

"What's up, buddy?" Max asked.

Christopher brushed his fingers across his cheeks, just in case there was any trace of his tears. "Nothing."

But Max's dark eyes lingered on him, and Christopher knew he knew. "Your brothers are up at the house with Jimmy," Max said. "I think they're trying to get him to let them keep a snake they found. He won't do it, of course. Jimmy's not much on snakes in the house."

"I can go on up and talk to them—"

"No," Max said. Without warning, he touched one finger to Christopher's cheek. His voice softened.

"They don't know what day it is, Christopher. It's not that they've forgotten. They just don't know."

Christopher nodded, ashamed at the tears welling in his eyes. He wished they would go away. He wished he would never cry again. He hated feeling so empty; he hated aching.

Max didn't question him. He looked out toward the main stables. "I thought we could saddle up a couple horses and take a ride down along the creek. Just the two of us. What do you think?"

"I guess—I guess that'd be okay."

He started to ask Max about the woman in the picture, about Calley, but he stopped himself. He knew Max wouldn't tell him. Max never talked about his life in New York before he'd come home to Wyoming to raise his orphaned half brothers. If he wanted to know about Calley, Christopher realized, he would have to find out on his own.

He promised himself he would. Somehow, some way, he was going to see his big brother smile as he had in those old pictures.

The key, he thought, was finding out who the dark-haired woman in the glasses was.

Calley. He had her first name.

But Calley who? How would he find her? And what would he tell her when he did?

Had she and Max been—

Christopher blushed, unable to finish the thought. He was still figuring out about girls and stuff.

Max glanced at him. "You okay?"

"Yep."

He would have to talk to his brothers. Together, they would come up with a plan.

Her name was Calley Hastings of New York, New York, and Christopher had her personal E-mail address. Next to horses, he was best at computers. Max had gotten him and his two little brothers a new computer for Christmas. Christopher figured if he worked at it, he could find anyone in the whole world.

Calley Hastings had been easy. He'd ventured back to the trunk in the storage room several more times, learning as much about her as he could.

Now he was ready. Timothy and Wynne were up in his room with him, hovering over the computer. Christopher had been careful with what he told them. Wynne especially had a big mouth.

He had to be careful with what he told Calley Hastings, too. If he said the wrong thing, he could scare her off. From what he'd gathered after sifting through the trunk, Max hadn't explained to her why he'd left New York. That was four years ago, but Calley Hastings might still hold a grudge. So, Christopher thought, he probably shouldn't pretend to be Max. And what if she were married? What if she had another boyfriend?

Christopher knew he was counting on Calley Hastings being just as unattached as his older brother, just as needful of smiling again as she had in the pictures in the trunk.

He wanted Calley Hastings to come to Wyoming.

But how would he get her here?

She would never come all the way to Wyoming to visit an eleven-year-old.

What to do?

"You going to stare at that computer all night?" Timothy asked impatiently.

Christopher sighed. He would type his message and think about it before sending it. That made sense to him. His poetry teacher had always told him to trust his instincts.

He shut his eyes, thinking.

Then he typed.

My name's Jill Baxter. I live on a ranch in Wyoming. I've been dreaming about New York since I was a little kid. I love the idea of all those tall buildings and all those people. I've always wanted to ride a subway.

Timothy squirmed next to him. "How come you're pretending to be a girl?"

Wynne screwed up his face as if he couldn't imagine such a thing.

Christopher shrugged. "It just feels right."

He continued, going with his instincts. He needed a cover story, a real tearjerker, if he had any hope of getting Calley Hastings to come out west.

I don't know if I'll ever get to New York. My husband died a few months ago. I'm here alone with the five kids and my grandmother. She's not well. The ranch takes up a lot of time and energy. Anyway, I don't want to burden you with my troubles. Can you tell me about New York City? Please. Tell me everything.

Christopher read back his work. It sounded pretty good to him. He would have to make the grandmother really sick, but he would wait until Calley Hastings wrote back. He didn't want to lay it on too thick right now, or she might get suspicious. In the meantime, he would have to think of a dramatic way for the husband to have died—maybe he would do something with tractors—and he would have to come up with ages for the five kids.

He hoped five kids weren't too many.

"Think it'll work?" Timothy asked.

Christopher grinned at his two brothers. "Trust me. Women love this stuff. It'll work."

"But she's a New Yorker."

"Yeah," Wynne said, as if he knew anything about the subject.

"Don't worry," Christopher said. "New Yorkers don't know anything about Wyoming."

Before long, though, he would have Calley Hastings on her way to Wyoming. He knew it.

# 1

---

*Black Creek Ranch, Wyoming*

Calley Hastings grimaced as she dumped her luggage at her feet just outside the Jackson Hole airport terminal. In another hour or so, she would be on a place called Black Creek Ranch. Her ride should be coming any minute. Her flight had been on time, but because she hadn't checked any luggage she didn't have to waste time at baggage claim. She had packed an efficient wardrobe into two carry-on bags, with the intention her stay in Wyoming not involve things like roping steer and sucking rattlesnake venom out of her bloodstream.

There was no turning back now. She had her pride. Before leaving New York, she'd learned the entire floor of her office building had a pool going for just how long she would last in Wyoming. Nobody, apparently, wanted to bet on the whole two weeks she'd arranged to be gone. If she'd been staying at a resort hotel in Jackson, maybe. But not out on some ranch. It was common knowledge that Calley Hastings liked concrete under her feet, doormen at her disposal, take-out gourmet in a pinch and Bergdorf-Goodman's anytime. If she felt the urge for fresh air and a view, she could have croissants on her building's rooftop deck. If she felt the urge for a taste of wildlife, she could head to the Bronx Zoo or go watch the pigeons in Central Park. She didn't have to fly all the way to Wyoming.

So why in blue blazes *had* she?

Hard to explain. Maybe impossible. But here she was.

The Grand Teton Mountains loomed all around her, the airport actually located on national parkland. She'd read about the Tetons in the Wyoming guide-book she'd picked up at a bookstore near her office. They were, she had to admit, stunningly beautiful, especially now that she'd landed safely in their midst. The small plane to which she'd transferred in Salt Lake City had tilted and dipped as if squeezing itself between the tall peaks, before coming to an abrupt halt on the short runway.

Calley liked big planes and big airports.

"It's a good thing I'm intrepid," she muttered to herself, as if saying the words would make it so.

Intrepid in New York was one thing. She knew her way around New York. Intrepid in Wyoming was an-other thing altogether. She'd noticed a stuffed cougar on display in the airport. It didn't bode well.

She didn't do cougars.

Although she'd been flying all day, the two-hour time difference between the East Coast and Wyoming meant it was just about sunset. The air was cool and dry, a refreshing break from the steamy Manhattan summer heat.

A dusty red pickup truck pulled up to the curb. Calley thought it might be her ride, someone dispatched from the ranch to pick her up. Jill Baxter surely couldn't travel. She had the five kids, the year-old twins were still too weak to leave home and her grandmother's Alzheimer's was worse. It wasn't easy for a young widow to run a Wyoming ranch on her own. Five kids and a dying grandmother didn't make the job any easier.

A tall man climbed from the truck, a dusty black cowboy hat hiding his face. He wore a blue denim shirt with the sleeves rolled up to the elbow, battered jeans and scarred cowboy boots, and the way he walked reminded Calley of Clint Eastwood in *The Good, the Bad and the Ugly,* which was as close as she'd ever gotten to the so-called Wild West.

The remaining light hit his face, and she gasped.

*Max.*

No. That was ridiculous. It couldn't be. Max Slade was more urban than she was. When he'd vanished, he'd vanished to Los Angeles or Miami or Chicago, even Paris. Not to Wyoming. Never mind the resemblance—the angular features, that straight line of a mouth—this guy looked as if he'd just been out hunting buffalo.

Calley was quite confident that all Max Slade had ever hunted were women.

While she struggled to control her shock, the man in the black cowboy hat—whoever he was—disappeared inside the terminal.

Calley jumped off the sidewalk and checked the license plate of the red truck. It featured a cowboy on a bucking bronco.

Definitely Wyoming plates.

The truck was too beat-up to be rented. She noticed a distinct weakening of her knees at the thought, however absurd, of seeing the man who'd left her high and dry four years ago. No one had ever hurt her as deeply as Max Slade.

Or ever would again.

She returned to her luggage, wondering where her ride was and trying to forget about the man in the black cowboy hat and his startling resemblance to that rat of her life, Max Slade.

The man emerged from the terminal two minutes later. Really, Calley thought, he couldn't be Max. This guy was more muscular, probably taller, and his was one grim mouth. Max Slade had liked to laugh. She had to give him that much.

He'd probably had a good laugh the day he'd squeegeed her out of his life.

The man removed his hat, an impatient hiss escaping that uncompromising, hard line of a mouth.

"Holy cow," Calley breathed.

He *was* Max Slade.

He turned. His eyes raked her from head to toe. He swore under his breath.

"Well, if it isn't Max Slade," Calley said with a small, utterly fake laugh. "Fancy meeting you here."

"It took some fancy doing, I'll say that." His voice sounded deeper, raspier than it had four years ago, and none too pleased. He nodded to his truck. "You can toss your stuff in back. We'll sort this thing out later."

Calley didn't move. She would grow roots and finish her days at the Jackson Hole airport before she tossed anything into the back of any truck owned by Max Slade. "I think you've made a mistake. There's nothing to sort out. I'm waiting for a ride—"

"I'm it."

"I don't think so."

"Calley, you've been had. I've been had. I'm your ride. Now, get in."

She shook her head. There had to be a Jill Baxter, a Black Creek Ranch, five kids, a dead husband, a dying grandmother. If Calley was anything, she was not gullible. Not after five months with Max Slade and seven years in New York. No, gullible was the *last* thing anyone would call Calley Hastings.

But a gnawing pain deep in the pit of her stomach suggested the possibility—the slim, awful chance—that he was telling the truth and she might indeed have been had.

Her only reasonable choice, however, was to blunder on. Every other choice involved trusting Max Slade, and that was unthinkable.

"Look, Max, I don't know what you're thinking, and I don't particularly care, but obviously you're mistaken. I'm waiting for a ride from someone from the Black Creek Ranch.''

''I know.''

His words—his arrogant tone—went right up her spine. ''You always were a know-it-all, Slade. Well, this time you're wrong. I'm staying with a woman named Jill Baxter. She's a young widow who's always wanted to see New York, but she's stranded out here in the wilds with five kids and a dying grandmother—''

''Calley, there is no Jill Baxter.''

She bristled. No. Forget it. Even if she *had* been had, she would stick to her story of a Jill Baxter and a Black Creek Ranch. Max didn't have to know how idiotic she'd been. He couldn't possibly know anything about what had brought her to Wyoming. After all, he must be here playing rancher himself at some dude ranch, participating in some urban-cowboy fantasy. She didn't know. She didn't *care*. She just wanted him on his way and herself back to New York.

''You could never admit to a mistake.'' She grabbed up a suitcase to channel some of her restless, unfocused energy. ''I don't know what weird set of coincidences brought us here at the same time and place, but *I'm* here to visit a friend and see her ranch—''

''Calley, I own Black Creek Ranch.''

She stared at him, speechless for perhaps the first time in her life. Even four years ago, when Max Slade had slithered out of her life for good, she hadn't been rendered speechless. Oh, indeed not. Anyone within earshot—even some who by no means should have been—had heard what she thought of him. As she re-called, she'd been articulate and inventive. Anger had been the only way she could protect her broken heart.

It was getting very dark. She was surrounded by mountains. She was on unfamiliar ground. Her state of affairs was getting worse by the minute. She had indeed, it seemed, succumbed to some kind of low, despicable scheme to lure her to Wyoming.

"You did this?" she managed to ask.

If possible, he looked even grimmer. "No."

"But you're telling me the truth? There's no Jill Baxter, no five kids, no dying grandmother? No dead husband?"

"Correct."

"But Black Creek Ranch—"

"It's real."

Her shoulders slumped.

"Look, you don't have much choice," Max said, not ungently. "It's tourist season here. You won't find a room, not this late. You might as well come on back to the ranch with me, and we'll sort this thing out."

"No way, Slade. I'm not going anywhere with you."

He shrugged. "Suit yourself."

Without another word, he went around to the driver's side of his truck, climbed in and started the engine.

Calley exhaled up at the sky. Lots of mountains. Lots of stars. Had *Max* cooked up Jill Baxter and the five kids and the dying grandmother and the horses Jill couldn't leave? She'd sounded so real, so believable. So lonely and desperate.

No, Max couldn't be behind the E-mail correspondence that had lured her out west. Max Slade could never pull off lonely and desperate.

So who had?

Even before she acknowledged what she was doing, Calley had hoisted up one of her overnight bags and heaved it into the back of Max Slade's truck. She grabbed the second one without hesitation, without thinking. If she *were* thinking, she would go back into the terminal, sleep on the floor and beg, borrow or steal her way onto the next flight out of Wyoming. It didn't even matter where it was headed. *Anywhere* that was flying distance away from Max Slade was fine with her.

But she flung open the passenger door and climbed up into his truck, refusing to look at Max as she more or less tripped up onto the seat. "I hate trucks," she said, staring straight ahead.

"Ever been in one?"

She gave him a cool look, repressing the outrageous, instantaneous, uncontrollable, *stupid* physical attraction she felt toward him. It had to be biological, she decided. Some chemical reaction. Like moths. "You know nothing about me, Max Slade. Nothing. So don't make assumptions."

He gave her a grudging smile that in no way reached his eyes. They were slate eyes, she remembered. Slate with flecks of black. Now they were lost in the night, in the shadows of his hat. "You always were such a bundle of sweetness and light. Relax. I'll have you in a warm bed in another hour or two." He paused, his smile vanishing. "Your own warm bed, of course."

Calley felt her throat go dry. She swallowed. It didn't help. Finally, she said, "Max, do you know what's going on?"

"Not exactly, but I have a feeling I know who does."

"Who?"

But he didn't answer her as he headed out into country she'd only seen in *National Geographic* and movies. She decided not to push Max for answers. Not right now. She was on his turf. In his *truck*, for heaven's sake. He was hardly a stranger, and even after four years and the horrible way he'd left her, she trusted him not to hurt her. But he wouldn't necessarily be above tossing her fanny out on the side of the road and letting her fend for herself if she annoyed him.

She glanced over at him. He was staring straight ahead, still grim faced. Well, the office pool back in New York couldn't have come up with this particular scenario as an option. She wasn't sure she believed it herself. Maybe she wasn't really here. Maybe she was back in New York and somebody had slipped something into her morning coffee and she was hallucinating.

Really, she thought. Max Slade in a cowboy hat. Max Slade living on a Wyoming ranch. Max Slade within two feet of her.

She *had* to be hallucinating.

But when he turned his gaze slightly from the straight, dark road and met her eyes, she knew she wasn't hallucinating or dreaming. Max Slade was real, and she was riding into the wilds of Wyoming with him.

# 2

They arrived at the ranch just before midnight. Max didn't try to put a better face on what had happened; he just let Calley Hastings adjust to her surroundings.

If that were possible, he thought, not optimistic.

Even with the array of stars overhead—nothing like she would ever see in New York—it was a dark night, none of the wild beauty of his corner of Wyoming visible. There were no streetlights out on Black Creek Ranch, no taxis to flag down should Calley change her mind about staying.

She climbed stiffly from the truck, not saying a word. If she were nervous, Max knew she wouldn't show it. He got one of her bags out of the back. She got the other. An owl hooted in the distance. He thought he saw her grimace.

Four years hadn't changed Calley Hastings a bit. She was still pretty and smart and of the opinion that life as she knew it ended west of the Hudson River, a city girl right down to her expensive imported undies. She didn't belong in Wyoming. Max had known that four years ago. That was why he'd left her in New York. His brothers—who had to be responsible for her presence—would see it the minute they laid eyes on her. Max still didn't know for sure how they'd lured Calley Hastings west. She wasn't talking. He suspected, however, it had something to do with the computer he'd bought them and their vivid imaginations.

Widows, dying grandmothers, a passel of kids. Max wasn't surprised Calley wasn't talking. She would hate having to admit she'd fallen for a sob story. Of course, he hadn't known a thing about any of it until he'd seen Calley Hastings standing at the airport.

He led her up onto the big front porch; all the old furniture—the rockers and swing and wicker settees—were no comfort, he suspected, to a woman accustomed to looking out at tall buildings. She wouldn't even be able to imagine the spectacular sunsets that spread out across the horizon beyond the porch, the wildlife that would amble through the meadows across the creek.

As he pushed open the front door, the light caught her face and shone on the intense blue eyes behind the stylish glasses. She didn't look afraid, he noted, or worried or particularly embarrassed. Instead, he thought she looked remarkably annoyed for a woman in her position.

Now *that*, he thought, was the Calley Hastings he'd known and maybe loved four years ago. She'd always grown irritated in the face of embarrassment, worry and even fear, and she was never, *ever* one to suffer

fools gladly, including when she was the one who was
the fool.

Jimmy Baxter was waiting up in the living room, the
biggest area in the rambling house. It had a huge stone
fireplace, an old player piano and lots of clunky,
comfortable furniture. Lissa Slade, the boys' mother,
had planned to redecorate the place. She'd never gotten the chance. So long as the furnishings didn't get
too tattered and remained vermin free, Max didn't
care. Decorating had been the least of his worries these
past four years.

Jimmy struggled to his feet. He had been a cowboy
most of his life, until a fall from a horse six years
ago—an ignominy he hated to acknowledge—had left
him with a permanent limp. Now he pretty much ran
the Slade household. He scanned Calley, his bushy
eyebrows rising as his dark, alert eyes turned to Max.
In that instant, Max knew, Jimmy had put the pieces
together and figured everything out—or at least as
much as he needed to know.

"Welcome," he said to Calley.

She nodded, her jaw clenched too tight for her to get
any words out. Max made the appropriate introduc-
tions, his own tone just this side of surly. What was he
going to do with Calley Hastings?

Get her back to New York as fast as he could.

"Once I figured out something was up, I set up the
downstairs bedroom," Jimmy told her. "It's got its
own bath. Figured you'd be more comfortable away
from the rest of the house. Anyway, I checked around

for spiders and snakes and the like, put clean towels in the bathroom, so it's all set.''

"Thank you," Calley said dryly.

"What about the boys?" Max asked.

Jimmy snorted. He was sinewy and well under six feet, not a hint of Mary Poppins about him. "Those rascals—they're up in bed.''

Calley narrowed her eyes. "Boys?"

Max grimaced. "Three boys. Christopher, Timothy and Wynne. They're the ones responsible for your being here.''

She was blinking rapidly, not understanding. And Calley Hastings was a woman who liked to understand, who prided herself on not diving headfirst into anything before she'd checked it out with her remarkable thoroughness and astuteness.

But she'd dived into this one, Max thought. No getting around it. No matter what kind of story the boys had cooked up, Calley couldn't claim to have been thorough or astute. If she had been, she would still be in New York.

"Are they—" She cleared her throat. "Are they yours?''

Max frowned. His what? Then Jimmy snorted, and Max knew. "Oh. No, they're not my sons. They're my brothers. Christopher's eleven, Timothy's nine and Wynne's six. I'm their legal guardian. They—" He sighed. He hadn't explained four years ago, and he couldn't now, not with Calley's very blue, very suspicious and distrusting eyes narrowed on him, not with Jimmy Baxter standing right there. "It's a long story.''

Jimmy mercifully intervened. "Warned you not to get those boys that damned computer, Max. They managed to order up a woman. Who knows what'll be next?"

Calley inhaled, saying nothing. Max understood. *Nobody* ordered up Calley Hastings. She was not just some woman to be manipulated, to have her sympathies played upon. No way. Calley was an individual to be taken seriously.

Max knew all about Calley Hastings's attitudes.

Jimmy continued to grumble, in no better mood than the Slade household's "surprise" guest. On a good day, Jimmy Baxter hated to be duped. This wasn't a good day. The boys hadn't just manipulated Calley Hastings; they'd also manipulated Max and even Jimmy. While the old cowboy was off running errands, the boys had grabbed Max and told him Jimmy needed a package picked up at the airport, saying that the shipping company was charging extra to have it driven out to the ranch. The request was unusual, but not unheard of.

With Jimmy not around for verification, Max had set off. He'd enjoyed the ride to Jackson. It had been a beautiful evening, the kind that had forced him to make peace with his life many long months ago. He'd finally accepted that he couldn't go back to New York. Even without the responsibility of Christopher, Timothy and Wynne, he couldn't go back. He wasn't the same man he'd been four years ago. Not just his life had changed. He had changed.

On that leisurely, pretty ride, he had never once considered that his bratty little brothers had conjured up one of his former love interests. They couldn't possibly have realized that of all the women he'd known, Calley Hastings was the most likely to skin him alive if she ever saw him again.

But when he'd seen her standing at the airport, a fish out of water, he'd guessed that was exactly what had happened. The rascals had lured Calley out to Wyoming. He would take their little deed up with them himself.

Right now, he had to deal with the immediate problem of Calley Hastings in his living room, but he knew there was nothing to be done tonight.

"Jimmy can show you to your room," he told her. "I'll see you in the morning. We'll figure out what to do then."

"Thank you. Good night."

Stiff. Formal. Max tried to smile. "Sleep well."

She gave him a look that suggested nothing would be as impossible as her sleeping well under his roof. But she went with Jimmy toward the back of the house, with Jimmy insisting, of course, on carrying both her bags, limp or no limp. Calley argued. Calley, Max remembered, *always* argued.

Max headed up the staircase off the front hall. As big as the house was, each boy had his own room. Jimmy had a small suite on the other side of the kitchen from Calley's room. Max and his brothers had the entire upstairs to themselves.

Feeling the fatigue of a long, bizarre day, he checked on them one by one, Wynne, the youngest, being first. He was snoring away, his army of stuffed animals tucked in around him. Max brushed his soft cheek.

Six years old and on his own. Hell, life just wasn't fair.

But he didn't dwell on the thought. He moved down the hall to Timothy's room. He had his covers kicked off, all sprawling arms and legs; he wasn't a chubby five-year-old anymore. He was nine and growing up fast.

Max felt his throat tighten. Time hadn't stopped the day their parents were killed. It kept marching along, one day after another, the little boys who'd been orphaned that horrible day vanishing, transforming, their loss and pain inexorably acting upon who they would become. Max ached for them. What would have become of them if their mother and father had lived? But Lissa and Ernest Slade were dead, and there was nothing Max could do to change that awful fact, nothing he could do to erase the effects of that tragedy from their children's lives.

He drew Timothy's blanket up over his skinny body. It was a cool night, quiet. Max tried not to imagine Calley Hastings downstairs, muttering to herself, trying to sort out what idiocy, what deviousness, had gotten her into this mess.

He wondered if she would go to bed before she'd double-checked every corner of her room for spiders and snakes.

Down the hall, Max stopped in Christopher's doorway. He was a serious boy, sensitive, introspective. He felt deeply the responsibility of passing on to his two younger brothers the memory of their parents. He could be as big a hellion as either Timothy or Wynne, no question of that, but his mischief was designed more to entertain and amuse, to distract, never to deliberately hurt.

He was trying for all the world to look as if he were dead to it, but Max knew better.

"A widow with five kids and a dying grandmother?" he asked.

Christopher stirred, opening his eyes. "Two of the kids are twins, just a year old. They were injured in the accident that killed the husband."

"What kind of accident?"

"Truck. They hit a moose."

"You're an imaginative kid, Chris, I'll say that. I can't believe Calley Hastings of all people bought such a sob story. Maybe you should be a writer when you grow up."

His eleven-year-old half brother brightened. "Then you're not mad?"

"Oh, *I'm* not mad," he said. "But before you breathe your sigh of relief, I suggest you wait until you meet Calley Hastings face-to-face."

Calley dreamed of rattlesnakes, big furry spiders and Max Slade, finally awakening to the pale light of dawn filtering through the muslin curtains and calamitous goings-on in the nearby kitchen. Three little boys. *What* was Max doing with three little brothers? How had he become their legal guardian? From the sounds coming through her door, she would have guessed an army of boys was in the kitchen, not just three.

She groaned, lying on her back. She hated morning. One eye focused on the old-fashioned clock on the chestnut washstand by her four-poster double bed. The little hand was on the five and the big was on the seven. By her calculations, that made the time five thirty-five and, therefore, still the middle of the night.

She exhaled at the ceiling. It was as if she were trapped in some bizarre mix of "My Three Sons" and "Bonanza." The entire all-male Slade household seemed to be up and at it at the crack of dawn. She heard voices. She heard a dog bark. She heard Jimmy Baxter growling and grumbling. She *might* have heard a rooster crowing. She was in Wyoming. She was not about to discount anything.

She smelled coffee. Surprisingly, her stomach growled. She hadn't eaten much on her trip west. She'd been too concerned with deciding how to greet the young widow who'd connected with her through a computer on-line service. What would they say to each other? How would they react face-to-face? Two women from two different worlds.

Not to worry, Calley thought. There was no widow, only Slades. Lucky her.

Well, the sooner up, the sooner out. With any luck, she would be back in New York by nightfall.

She threw back her covers, which consisted of two hand-stitched quilts, and crawled stiffly from the bed. The guest room was spacious and airy, with antique furnishings, cream-colored walls and two windows that looked out on God-knew-what. Calley padded across the thickly braided rug and pulled open the curtains.

The view was glorious. Utterly breathtaking. Better than "Bonanza" reruns, she thought. Rolling pastures, a winding creek, clusters of trees, grazing horses and huge mountain peaks rising up all around the narrow valley. It was just the sort of view she'd imagined when she'd encountered "Jill Baxter's" first E-mail message and found herself captivated by the very idea of Wyoming, and by how very different Jill Baxter's life must be from her own.

"So," she muttered under her breath. "Yesterday wasn't some weird dream."

She felt like Dorothy waking up way the hell over the rainbow. And like Dorothy, pretty as Wyoming was, it wasn't home. Not hers, anyway. It was Max Slade's home, strange as that idea was. She had to get straight in her head the simple fact that the man she'd met last night was the same Max Slade who'd exited from her life without a note, a phone call, a fax, even a message left with her doorman. This Max Slade came with a cowboy hat, scruffy cowboy boots, a ranch and three small boys. Her Max Slade had been the ultimate urban male. But the two men were one and the same.

Perhaps it was reasonable after all, Calley decided, to find him living among rattlesnakes.

She quickly retreated to the adjoining bathroom, done completely in white and not as old-fashioned as the bedroom, but hardly new. A small window looked out on a barn of some sort. Postcard country. She felt an unexpected tug of regret at not being able to explore it. Well, there was nothing to be done about it. She didn't want to stay in the same city as Max Slade, much less the same house. She would pick up a few postcards at the airport on her way back east.

*Nobody* back in New York needed to know she'd encountered her ex-lover instead of a lonely young widow with fantasies of life in New York.

Calley showered and changed into a plain white T-shirt, jeans that had nothing of the West in their cut and her New York Knicks sweatshirt. No pretending *she* wasn't from the Big Apple.

Taking a deep breath, she opened the door to the hall.

A little boy of about six was standing practically on the threshold, his unexpected presence giving Calley a start. She didn't scream. Years of negotiating the New York subway system had taught her to stay on the alert and not overreact, screaming only when she had good reason to scream. Presumably a six-year-old wasn't good reason.

He had tawny hair that needed cutting, huge blue eyes and two missing baby teeth. He wore shorts and a Spiderman sweatshirt, no shoes. Optimistic about the weather, it seemed. A scrawny, threadbare, stuffed golden retriever puppy was slung over one shoulder, and he had a plastic cup in one hand.

Max was this child's legal guardian, she thought. How? Why? She shook off the rush of questions. Answers would have to come later, if ever. What had become of Max Slade was simply none of her business. He'd seen to that.

Calley peered into the cup, noting the contents looked suspiciously like dead flies. "What's that?" she asked.

"Dead flies."

She made a face. "Charming."

He grinned, delighted with her reaction. At that moment, Max came up behind him. In the pale light of morning, he looked rugged and very Clint Eastwood. "They're not real," he said.

"Oh." Calley manufactured a smile. "I knew that."

"This is my brother Wynne. Wynne, this is Calley Hastings. She's from New York City." As if that explained any peculiarities the boy might notice about her.

"Nice to meet you," Wynne Slade said, racing down the hall before Calley could respond.

Max glanced after him. "Wait'll you see his rubber snake collection."

"Cute kid," Calley said, tongue in cheek.

"He loves practical jokes and has a hell of a temper. Too used to getting his own way, I guess. Don't let him fool you, he's a mushball inside. Doesn't go anywhere without his puppy." Max's searing slate eyes turned back to her. "You look like you could use a pot or two of coffee. Come on. Jimmy's cooking breakfast.''

Despite her years in New York as a professional, Calley had to admit to her uneasiness as she followed Max into a huge country kitchen, where an entourage of dogs and boys seemed to be competing for volume. So far as she could tell, Jimmy Baxter made no distinction between dogs and boys, yelling at them all in the same gruff way as he flipped pancakes on a griddle and waved his spatula in mock warning.

The oldest boy was setting the table, a long, rectangular slab of pine situated in front of a double window overlooking the backyard. He eyed Calley with a mixture of curiosity and nervousness, his cheeks flushed. Max introduced him as Christopher Slade. He just gave her an embarrassed smile in greeting. Calley guessed he'd been the mastermind of the sob story that had successfully lured her to Wyoming. She wondered if he had any idea he'd accomplished no small feat or simply assumed she was a gullible, idiotic New Yorker, no match for a determined eleven-year-old Westerner with a vivid imagination.

The middle boy—lanky and probably a lot cuter than any nine-year-old male would want to admit being—was obeying Jimmy's command to let the dogs out before he threw them on the griddle, too.

"That's Timothy," Max said. "From what I can gather, the year-old twins were his contribution to the Jill Baxter tale. Wynne helped think up their names."

Alex and Jason, as Calley recalled. She didn't mention the little stuffed mice she'd tucked in her suitcase for them. She would prefer Max not know just how oblivious she'd been to his brothers' hoax. Talk about walking into the lion's mouth.

Duped by three boys, never mind that they were Slades. It was mortifying. She prided herself on being savvy and sophisticated, wise to every trick in the book, and here she'd fallen for a loony story off a computer network, one worthy of convicted con men. What had the little monsters been thinking? A dying grandmother. Five kids. A widow. What lurid imaginations.

"I've already had breakfast," Max told her, his tone brusque, his eyes not reaching hers. He seemed even more distant and grim than he had the night before. "I need to get some work done before I drive you back into Jackson. There's a flight out around noon. I checked."

The three Slade boys grew silent. Calley nodded, not sure what she should say. On the one hand, she didn't want to get the boys into any more hot water than they must already be in. On the other hand, she couldn't wait to beat a path out of Max Slade's presence.

He retreated out the back door with the last of the dogs.

"Let's eat," Jimmy said.

He served up platters of pancakes and ham, and produced a pitcher of hot maple syrup, his gruff manner a welcome counter to the awkwardness of the moment. He pointed out the coffeepot and open shelf where he kept the mugs, and Calley gratefully helped herself. She was aware of three sets of Slade eyes on her. They were assessing her, waiting, trying to predict what she might do.

Finally, Jimmy sighed, muttering something about having eaten with Max, and made his exit, too.

"We had to lie," Christopher Slade announced once Jimmy was safely out of earshot.

Timothy concurred. "We knew you'd never come if we didn't."

"Yeah," Wynne said, as if he understood what his older brothers were talking about. He'd set his cup of "dead flies" next to his plate of pancakes, which he was drowning in syrup.

Calley sat at the long, scarred pine table with her mug of steaming coffee. Really, having to think at this hour was beyond the call of duty. "I'm sure you meant well."

Actually, she wasn't. They were Slades, after all, and who knew how young a Slade started with his nefarious ways? For all she knew, scheming was a genetic thing with them.

Christopher hadn't touched the pancakes and ham he'd heaped onto his plate. He seemed more serious than the other two, his eyes nearly as penetrating as his older brother's. "Max dumped you because of us."

"Is that what you think?" Calley asked.

"It's true."

"No, it's not true. Max dumped me because he's a—"

She stopped herself. She'd intended to say "heel." It was more restrained than most of the names she'd come up with in the past four years to describe Max

Slade. But these were his brothers. They must look up to him. He was responsible for them. She bought herself a few seconds by forking a couple of pancakes onto her plate. Jimmy Baxter had fixed more than three boys and one woman could consume in a week, never mind one morning. Suddenly, she was ravenous.

But she made herself explain. "Your brother and I went our separate ways quite some time ago. It had nothing to do with you."

"It did," Christopher said, his tone grave for an eleven-year-old. "Max left New York and came back here to take care of us when our parents were killed."

Calley nearly dropped the platter of ham. She glanced at Wynne, who was digging into his pancakes, disengaging himself from the conversation. Her throat had tightened. It was all making sense. These boys were orphans. Their mother and father were dead. Max had mentioned none of this last night on the drive to the Slade ranch.

Christopher and Timothy were studying her closely, as if they dared not anticipate what she might do. She was a woman, a New Yorker, and for the past six weeks, they'd had her believing in a character worthy of a daytime drama. The conniving little rats. They'd been so believable.

What was she supposed to say to three orphans?

She was a financial planner. She knew money, not little boys. Nevertheless, they had to know how wrong they were. Max hadn't abandoned her because of their parents' deaths. He'd abandoned her because he was a womanizing bastard afraid of commitment. He and Calley had started talking around, if not actually *about,* a life together—marriage, an apartment on Central Park—then he'd bailed out.

*That* was what had happened.

But none of her scenarios for how the notorious Max Slade had ended up after their affair remotely put him on a Wyoming horse ranch raising three orphaned half brothers. In the pits of hell, yes. Staked to a hill of fire ants, absolutely. Hopelessly in love with a woman who wouldn't give him the time of day, by all means. But not in Wyoming with three kids.

"Look," Calley said, trying not to get too far ahead of herself, "I'm not angry with you. I'm sure you had your reasons for doing what you did. I'm surprised I fell for your story, that's all. I'm not known for being gullible—"

"What's gullible?" Wynne asked.

"A sucker," Christopher said.

Calley made a face. Well, why mince words? "Anyway, obviously I fell for your story hook, line and sinker. I guess I must have been bored, ready for an adventure—I don't know. I should have checked out this Jill Baxter. I really don't know why I didn't. But I didn't, and now here I am. It's just one of those things."

None of the boys responded. Calley tried her pancakes, which to her surprise were multigrain. Jimmy Baxter perhaps wasn't as oblivious to good nutrition as she'd anticipated. And the syrup was sweet, heavenly.

Timothy fastened his especially intense blue eyes on her. "Then you're leaving for sure?"

"For sure," she said.

Wynne pushed out his lower lip, looking even younger than six. "I want you to stay."

Christopher leaned back in his chair, his eyes narrowed, his feelings unreadable. *He* looked older than his eleven years, that know-it-all expression all too reminiscent of his older brother's. The Slade genes at work. "If there's nothing between you and Max, why can't you stay?"

"Because I'm here under false pretenses—"

"Not anymore."

She swallowed a mouthful of pancakes. Explaining the nuances of her relationship with Max to his kid brothers was out of the question. She did have some dignity left. "I can't stay."

"You bought a round-trip ticket. You said so in your last E-mail."

As if she needed reminding. It was embarrassing to think how much these kids knew about her, things *she'd* told *them*. "I can change it."

Wynne's shoulders drooped. "I want you to stay," he repeated as if he were well accustomed to getting what he wanted. Calley had no illusions he'd become attached to her in the past half hour; he was just a sociable little kid who liked having company. Her arrival probably broke up the monotony of life on a Wyoming ranch.

"What will you do in New York?" Timothy asked.

"This is your vacation," Christopher added.

Calley was well aware she had taken two weeks of her vacation to visit a trapped, lonely woman who'd always wanted to come to New York and, Jill Baxter's circumstances being what they were, likely never would. Something in their weeks-long computer correspondence had touched a nerve with her. She couldn't precisely say what it was, but she wasn't ready to dismiss it. Had the younger Slade brothers revealed some of their own yearnings in their messages to her? Or were Christopher, Timothy and Wynne Slade so devious they could fake the emotion that finally had prompted her to book a flight to Wyoming?

She would be wise, she knew, not to project any emotions or motivations onto anyone with Slade blood running in his veins. Wariness was in order.

Yet the boys' desire to have her stay seemed sincere, regardless of its motivation. They'd gone through a lot of trouble to get her here. Clearly they'd misunderstood her relationship with their older brother and guardian, creating their own fantasy of why it had ended. Perhaps if she stayed, at least for a day or two, they could see for themselves the reality of her and Max Slade. The truth was, even if he'd dumped her because of the tragic turn of events in his half brothers' lives, he could have gotten word to her. He could have told her what had happened. Instead, he'd used the tragedy as an excuse to rid her from his life and had left her without so much as a goodbye.

It wasn't Max who'd lured her to Wyoming, either. It was his brothers. Something she definitely needed to remember. Max Slade no more wanted her back in his life than she wanted to be in it.

But she found herself saying, "I'll pour myself another cup of coffee, and you boys can show me around. Then I'll make up my mind." She studied each boy in turn. Good-looking kids, trying to figure her out the same way she was trying to figure them out. She had to remember to remain on her guard. "Just one thing. Keep me away from anything that crawls or slithers."

Wynne's expressive eyes widened. "What's that mean?"

Chris grinned. "It means she doesn't want to see Fred."

Fred? Who the hell was Fred?

More to the point, *what* was he?

But none of the boys was talking. Calley refilled her mug. Yep, these rascals were Slades. Best to stay on her toes at all times, no matter how long she stayed.

# 3

Max didn't need to do as much as he did on the ranch. He had plenty of help and plenty of money to hire more if he needed it. Black Creek was not a struggling ranch. The Slades hadn't been poor in over a century. But work set an example for his younger brothers, and it helped keep his own demons at bay.

Out on the land, he could forget the dreams he'd had as an eleven-year-old like Christopher, because the land had never been the problem, never the reason he'd wanted to leave Wyoming at the first opportunity.

Out on the land he could remember that he belonged here, with Christopher, Timothy and Wynne. He could remember that this was his home. This was what held meaning in his life. Not New York, not even the woman he'd loved and left there. That was something his brothers needed to understand, Calley Hastings or no Calley Hastings. He'd made his decision four years ago. It was the most painful decision he'd ever made in his life, but it had been the right one.

Regardless, there was no going back.

When he returned to the house, he spotted Calley. He started to call to her, but stopped when he realized she was standing rock still. He expected a rattlesnake, something dangerous and unfamiliar to her, and approached her carefully, not wanting to spook her or whatever had her white-faced and scared. It could just be Fred, the boys' "pet" snake, but Fred was nonpoisonous. Still, Calley might not know that. She was a New Yorker, after all. She knew her roaches, rats, pigeons, not necessarily her snakes.

He brushed the dust off his denim shirt, felt his fatigue despite the early hour. It had been four years since he'd loved and lost his smart, high-strung, blue-eyed Calley Hastings. It seemed more like ten years ago, a hundred even. He felt so much older, so much more experienced, so damned different.

His gaze fell to her rounded bottom, encased in what appeared to be brand-new jeans. He smiled. Then again, it could have been just yesterday that he'd had Calley Hasting in bed with him.

She had to have heard his approach. But she didn't turn around. Didn't, so far as he could see, move a muscle.

He glanced around the lawn and the dirt driveway, but saw no snake, poisonous or otherwise. "What's the matter, has Wyoming frozen you to the ground?"

"Shh," she hissed, still not moving.

"Calley—"

Then he saw. Lucky, the household pet turkey, stood in the shade of the henhouse about three yards off, his beady eyes pinned on the Slade household's new guest. The fowl had her in a standoff. She didn't move. He didn't move.

Max held back a howl of laughter.

"Does he bite?" Calley asked, her voice just above a whisper. *She* wasn't about to laugh.

"He never has, but he doesn't see that many New Yorkers." Max went up beside her, noting that she kept her eyes on the bird. He suppressed a smile. "Lucky, meet Calley Hastings. Calley, meet Lucky."

"He's harmless?"

"Utterly."

Her rigid body went slack. "Well, I'm not about to shake hands or whatever with some stupid turkey. He can just go on his way or do whatever it is turkeys do. I'm not—" She broke off, making a face. "I suppose I'll have to brush up on my barnyard etiquette."

Max laughed, clapping his hands a couple of times. Lucky got the message and strutted off as if he owned the place, something no one on Black Creek Ranch would bother arguing. "Never figured a wily New Yorker like you would be afraid of a turkey."

"Turkeys can be mean."

"How do you know?"

"I read it somewhere."

Or she'd made it up. Calley Hastings wasn't above making up facts to win an argument or avoid humiliation. Max decided not to press her for details. "Well, Lucky's not mean. He's just wary of strangers. I don't think he'd hurt you."

"What're you doing with a pet turkey?"

"He was destined for the oven a couple Thanksgivings ago, but the boys protested, and I relented. Now he's part of the family."

Calley eyed him dubiously. "The dogs don't bother him?"

"Nobody bothers Lucky."

"Kids and animals." She sighed, regaining her composure now that the "crisis" had passed. "I don't know what I'm doing here. I gather Lucky has the run of the place?"

"Not as much as he thinks. Jimmy and I both balked at letting him in the house. He likes playing Frisbee with the boys. He's gotten pretty good at catching it. Better than Wynne, actually."

Calley turned and faced him, her arms folded under her breasts. She still had on her Knicks sweatshirt, despite the fast-rising temperature. Her expression, at best, was highly dubious. "A Frisbee-playing turkey? Right. Very funny. Well, you're not going to have *that* laugh at my expense. I'm not falling for that one."

"He goes sledding with the boys in the winter, too. He likes being the last one aboard."

She snorted in disbelief.

"It's true," Max said.

"Well, I gotta tell you, Max, after what you Slade boys pulled on me, I'm not going to believe anything that comes out of the mouth of a single one of you without tangible proof. You get a Frisbee and toss it to the turkey. If the turkey catches it, then I'll believe you."

He shrugged. "Okay. Maybe the boys'll be up for a game before you go."

"Oh." Her cheeks colored suddenly, very unlike Calley Hastings, who could hold her own in any office on Wall Street. "Then you haven't talked to them. They—we—I decided to stay on awhile. A few days, anyway."

Max narrowed his eyes on her. She seemed sincere, even ill at ease. "They come up with another sob story?"

"No."

"Then what? You can't *want* to stay, not with me here."

There wasn't a hint of self-pity in his tone. He was simply stating the facts. He'd seen Calley's face when she'd recognized him at the airport last night. She'd thought she'd landed in hell instead of Jackson Hole, Wyoming. He knew he'd done her wrong four years ago. Without doubt, so did she. And Calley Hastings wasn't known for forgiving and forgetting.

"I wouldn't want to stay in the same state with you, Max Slade," she went on. "But that's not the point. Or maybe it is the point. Your brothers went through a great deal of trouble to find me and get me here. They need to see that we're not suited for each other. They need to understand we wouldn't have worked out whether or not they'd been orphaned. Right now, they're convinced we'd be happily married or something if only you hadn't had to come out here to raise them. They blame themselves for what happened between us four years ago."

"It's not their fault."

"Oh, I know that." She gave him a cool look, nothing in her expression indicating she had any doubt her opinion of him needed revising. "I think if I stay on here for a few days, they'll know it, too."

Max shook his head. "No, Calley. You're leaving today. What those boys think or don't think is no concern of yours. I'm not going to fight with you for the next two weeks just to prove to my brothers they aren't responsible for what happened between us."

"I never said I'd stay the entire two weeks. At the rate we're going, they'll see our point in about forty-eight hours." She dropped her arms to her sides, the morning sun glistening on her dark, shiny hair. "Anyway, I'm not suggesting we have to fight to make them see what we felt for each other four years ago can't be reignited. We can be civil and accomplish that. I mean, even three boys under the age of thirteen ought to be able to see there're no sparks between us."

Max regarded her a long moment. "No sparks whatsoever?"

"Correct. None."

She pushed her glasses up, her eyes, intense and very blue, on him. Max didn't know if what he was feeling was a "spark," but it damned sure was something. Would the boys see it? Would Calley? He shook off the thought. Who saw what, what he felt—it was all irrelevant. She was leaving. He would drive her to Jackson, put her on a plane and wave goodbye to her forever.

"I know you'd like to think I've been languishing in your absence the past four years, Max," she said airily. "But the fact is, I haven't been. Not at all."

Max wondered if she was protesting too much, *knew* he'd hurt her. But Calley had never been one to like admitting to being hurt.

"Christopher assured me you're unattached. He says you confided as much in your messages to him."

She sniffed, possibly in an attempt to hide her embarrassment over what else she might have confided to his half brothers. "'Unattached' doesn't mean desperate, and I'd have to be desperate to want you back in my life."

Max grinned. "Wish old Lucky knew how tough you are. He'd never have tried to intimidate you."

"Don't make fun of me, Max Slade. And don't stand there and pretend you want me in your life any more than I want you in mine, because you don't. You're just—well, I guess you don't see many women out here in the wilds of Wyoming, and you're just responding accordingly to one in your presence."

That much he couldn't deny. She was a woman in his midst, and he was definitely responding.

She thrust her hands onto her hips. "But don't go thinking I'm going to mistake lust for anything but lust. I did that once with you and lived to regret it. It won't happen again."

In that instant, Max saw the consequences of what he'd done four years ago. The choice he'd made—the only one he'd been capable of making at the time—had had a lasting effect on her. Because of him, Calley Hastings would never easily trust her judgment of a man again, if at all.

"Do you regret what we had together, Calley?" he asked softly, suddenly serious.

He watched her throat as she swallowed, her icy blue eyes on him. She didn't answer at once. The light breeze caught her hair as fresh color brightened her cheeks. Finally, she shook her head. "No. I don't regret what I *thought* we had. I guess I don't even regret what we did have. I learned from it. I'm not the same woman I was four years ago, Max." She swallowed again, biting down on her lower lip. "Forget that at your own peril."

"Understood."

"I'll go pack," she said, and marched back toward the house.

Max didn't stop her. She should pack. He should drive her to the airport so she could catch the noon flight out. Then he could sit down with Christopher, Timothy and Wynne and explain to them that while he and Calley Hastings had once loved each other, that love was in the past. It was a conditional love, the kind that could go away. It wasn't like the unconditional love he had for them, the kind that could never go away. He would explain, and eventually, they would understand.

But Calley Hastings would be gone.

And suddenly, he wasn't sure he could bear that, not twice in one lifetime.

* * *

Max loomed in the guest-room doorway as Calley zipped her leather suitcase shut on the quilt-covered double bed. She wasn't looking at him, but she knew he was there.

"All right," he said. "You can stay."

She whipped around and glared at him, wishing she didn't notice every damned thing there was to notice about him, from his sun-washed dark hair to his scruffy, sexy cowboy boots. Earlier, when she'd caught him out of the corner of her eye, looking all dusty and rugged, she'd almost reacted, which would have surely incited the turkey. But she'd come to her senses since then. She was getting out of Wyoming. It had been madness to think she could stay.

"I have no intention of staying," she told him.

He frowned. "You just said—"

"I must have had some kind of lapse facing down that turkey. Staying out here in the wilds with you one *hour* longer than I have to is—well, it's crazy." She hefted her suitcase off the bed and dropped it to the floor. "But mercifully, I've come to my senses."

His eyes narrowed on her, as if he knew more about what she was thinking than she did. "So there are still sparks between us."

"Let's just say I'm not neutral on the subject of Max Slade and probably never will be."

Crossing his arms on his chest, he leaned against the doorjamb, one knee bent, eyes still narrowed. Calley shuddered inwardly. Nope. She was definitely not neutral when it came to Max Slade. If she stayed, his brothers would see that. There would be no pretense of bygones being bygones. It wasn't that her feelings for Max could be reignited. It was that they were still smoldering, hot embers buried deep inside her that she couldn't quite stomp out. She could feel them threatening to explode into an uncontrollable wildfire, their flames consuming her and all she'd become in the past four years.

Best to head back to New York.

"All the more reason you should stay," Max said finally.

She blinked at him. "Beg your pardon?"

"Your lack of neutrality on me is getting in your way. You need to get me out of your system so you can move on with your life."

"Get you out of my system—move on—where did you ever—"

She gulped for air, sputtering. Nobody had ever, ever jerked her chain the way Max Slade did. He could take her from calm, cool and collected to enraged in seconds.

And not just enraged.

But she couldn't think about that right now.

"Of all the arrogance," she said. "I *have* moved on with my life."

"Then why are you here?"

"Because I'm a sap. Because I've been working too hard and was ripe for an adventure. Believe me, if I knew I'd find you on the western horizon, I'd never have boarded the plane yesterday."

He shook his head knowingly. "You're here, Calley, because there's a hole in your life that you were hoping this trip would fill."

"There are no holes in my life. I love New York. I love my job. I have great friends. I have a great apartment. I'm happy. I'm here because I fell for your brothers' elaborate sob story and because Wyoming sounded like a good place for a summer vacation. That's *it*."

Max was unmoved. "You've got plenty of money. You could have booked a room at one of the nice hotels in Jackson. You could have done Wyoming without the widow, the five kids or the dying grandmother."

"Well, so you've seen my soft side. You might not remember me this way, Max, but I'm a nice person. At least, I try to be."

"Stay, Calley."

His voice was quiet, deep, irresistible. If she let it, it could knock her off her feet. It could make her remember what Max Slade had once meant to her. His humor, his steadiness, his confidence.

She shook her head adamantly. She *had* to go.

Max frowned. "You'd decided to stay. What changed your mind?"

"Going eyeball to eyeball with a turkey, I guess."

He smiled, not buying her answer. "I don't think so."

"Oh, and you know my mind better than I do?"

"I didn't say that. I just don't think you're being honest with yourself. Or me. Lucky had nothing to do with changing your mind, and you know it."

Calley grabbed both suitcases. Maybe Jimmy Baxter could drive her to the airport. Maybe she wouldn't have to go with Max. He didn't budge from the doorway, never mind that she couldn't get through with both suitcases.

"Admit it, Calley," he said.

"Admit what?"

"It wasn't Lucky that changed your mind."

She let the suitcases drop to the floor. "All right. I admit it. It wasn't Lucky. It was simply an assault of common sense."

He drew away from the door, walking toward her in that young Clint Eastwood way of his. Using one heel, he gently kicked the door shut behind him, not slackening his pace. Calley tried to look nonchalant. What did she care if Max Slade shut the door and was moving in on her? He was nothing to her. All that stuff about hot embers and wildfires was just an overreaction. So he was as physically attractive as ever. More so, even. So what? That was just lust. She'd learned not to succumb to lust. Her emotions, her *soul,* had to be involved. And they weren't, not with Max Slade. Not anymore.

He stopped right in front of her, the toes of his boots not two inches from the toes of her sneakers.

She could see the fine lines at the corners of his eyes, no doubt from the Wyoming wind and sun and, perhaps, the responsibility of raising his three small brothers. His skin was tanned, more weather-beaten than it had been in New York. The muscles in his chest and arms looked more developed, hardened by physical work, not hours in the gym. She noticed scars and calluses and a roughness that hadn't been there four years ago. He wasn't the same man who'd brought her flowers and silly gifts, who'd loved the pulse of New York as much as she did. She'd come to love that Max Slade, then to hate him.

But he'd changed, hardened, and maybe she didn't know this Max Slade at all.

He touched one finger to the corner of her mouth. She didn't draw back. Instead, she stood rock still and let the effects of his touch spin right down to her toes. She remembered the dozens—the hundreds—of dreams she'd had about feeling Max Slade's touch again, feeling his mouth on her, his body inside her.

Everything had changed when he'd disappeared. Everything. It didn't matter why.

"It wasn't an assault of common sense that changed your mind, either," he said softly. "It was more like an assault of all your senses."

"Max . . ."

"Wasn't it, Calley?"

She swallowed, shutting her eyes. His lips followed where his finger had been, just at the corner of her mouth, a kiss so feathery and light she wondered if she might possibly be imagining it. But she inhaled, her lips parting slightly, and his mouth came down full on hers, deepening their kiss, ending any doubt that it might just be her imagination. She had to pull away.

But she didn't. This was the Max she remembered, the Max she'd once loved. However he had changed, he was still the same man.

"Tell me the truth," Max whispered against her mouth. "Tell yourself."

"The truth. Right."

Her body was awash in sensations she hadn't felt in a long time, maybe too long. No one had ever made her feel the way Max Slade did. He made her ache for him, want him, need him. They were feelings she'd learned to distrust. Aching, wanting, needing. They weren't emotions she wanted to feel.

She pushed herself away from him, nearly tripping over a suitcase. "The truth is, I've lost my damned mind."

Something she couldn't read flashed in those searing slate eyes. Then it was gone, even faster than it had appeared. In someone else, it might have been disappointment. In Max Slade, it could be anything. She wouldn't even try to guess what was going on in his mind.

His expression turned hard, pragmatic. "I'll get the truck started and meet you out front."

"Oh, no, you don't. I'm staying."

He gritted his teeth. "That's it, Calley. I'm staking you out for the cougars. There's no making sense of you."

She ignored him, hoisting up first one suitcase and then the other back onto the bed. It was all so very clear to her now. She knew exactly what she was doing. "I'm not going back to New York with you thinking I'm running from you. Hell, no. I'm staying here and *proving* to you, Max Slade, that you don't mean a damned thing to me anymore. And I'm not leaving until you admit there's one woman on the face of the earth that doesn't give a rat's hind end about you. And that woman is me."

"Well," he said with surprising equanimity, "suit yourself."

"I will."

"Okay. Lunch is at noon. I'll tell Jimmy to set you a place."

"Fine."

"In the meantime, might as well make yourself at home."

"Oh, sure," she grumbled under her breath. "That ought to be easy. Kids, turkeys, horses, cowboys, mountains. Just what I'm used to."

Max regarded her with amusement. "It's going to be a fun two weeks, Calley."

"Two weeks? Who said anything about two weeks? This is a day-by-day thing."

"No, it's not."

"The devil—"

He started to leave, his back to her. "It's two weeks, Calley, just like it says on your ticket. I've got work to do. I can't be wondering every day if you're leaving or staying. You made your decision. You're staying." He turned back to her, his eyes unreadable. "I'm off for the afternoon. I'll see you when I see you."

She folded her arms under her breasts. "Makes no difference to me when I see you."

"I remain to be convinced."

# 4

"Is Max very different from when you knew him?" Christopher Slade asked as he and Calley walked up a dirt path behind the stable.

She gave a small, evasive shrug, pleading ignorance. It was a warm afternoon, the temperature having climbed considerably since morning, but the dry air kept her from feeling the heat. Timothy and Wynne had long abandoned them on her whirlwind tour of Black Creek Ranch—or at least what they could get to on foot. Evidently, its acreage included far more than a couple hours of wandering could take in. But what Calley had seen surpassed even her highest hopes of raw Western majesty and beauty.

Either that or she was so fresh out of a dirty Manhattan subway she simply didn't see the region's physical shortcomings. Its social shortcomings were obvious: only Slades, hired hands, Jimmy Baxter, assorted dogs, horses, chickens, wild animals and one Frisbee-playing turkey for company. In short, there wasn't a thing to do on Black Creek Ranch that didn't involve the elements or wildlife. She hadn't dared ask for the location of the nearest movie theater.

Given Christopher's heroic, if underhanded, efforts to get her to come west, Calley decided she owed him a direct answer. "I haven't seen enough of Max to know if he's any different."

"I think he is."

"Why's that?"

He thought a moment. His eyes were lost beneath his San Francisco Giants baseball cap. Now San Francisco, Calley thought, was her idea of life west of the Mississippi. Christopher had mentioned that Max promised to take him to a game before the end of the season. She suspected the oldest of Max Slade's three half brothers had a sensitivity to the world around him that wouldn't always make life easy for him on Black Creek Ranch.

On their afternoon walk, he'd pointed out things Timothy and Wynne had bypassed. It wasn't a matter of age, but of sensibility. A flowering tree their mother had planted now grown to maturity, a colt whose birth he and Max and Jimmy Baxter had overseen one cold, dark night, a hawk on the horizon. They were what Christopher Slade noticed. He was a good-looking kid, strong for his age, and Calley would bet he would do just fine with the junior-high girls come September. His sensitivity didn't make him less of a Slade.

"I found some pictures of you and Max." He walked ahead of her, not glancing back as he spoke. "They're what got me looking for you. He seemed happier then."

"Well, he was younger."

"Not that much."

Calley followed him into the shade of a huge oak at the corner of the main stable, an impressive structure of stone and wood. "You've got to be the first eleven-year-old I've ever met who doesn't think thirty's ancient."

Not that she knew many eleven-year-olds. None, in fact. Her life in New York didn't put her in touch with many kids. But she wasn't going to tell Christopher, lest he get any fresh ideas about throwing her ignorance up in her face and manipulating her into doing something else stupid. So far, she had a poor record. Coming to Wyoming had been yesterday's stupidity. Kissing Max Slade had been today's.

"Were you and Max happy?" Christopher asked, briefly glancing back at her in the shade of the oak. Her lame attempt at levity hadn't produced any sign of humor or amusement in him. "I mean, do you think you'd be together still if he'd stayed in New York?"

Calley sighed. There was nothing to do but be straight up with the kid. "When we were seeing each other, yes, I guess you could say we were happy. But that was quite a while ago. We went our separate ways four years ago, Christopher."

"Because of us."

"Not because of you. If Max and I were meant to be together, he would have told me about your parents. Anyway, it doesn't matter why we're not together, not anymore. We're not, and we've both gone on with our lives. Maybe when you're older, you'll understand—"

Christopher stopped, turning to her in the middle of the dirt path. "I understand now."

Caught, she thought. She'd patronized him, and he'd just called her on it. She'd hated being reminded she was a kid at age eleven, too. "I'm sorry. It's just not easy for me to discuss private matters."

He gave her a small, self-deprecating grin. "You mean it's none of my business?"

She smiled. "You're a smart kid, Christopher Slade."

"Yep," he said.

"Then you know you can't make two people feel what they don't feel."

He shook his head, not so much in disagreement, Calley thought, as amazement that she just didn't get it. She had the feeling he thought he was dealing with a complete moron. "Max left New York for us. He left you for us. He hasn't had any other girlfriends in four years. I want— He deserves—" But Christopher stopped in frustration, his age catching up with him. "I can't explain."

A sensitive kid, Calley thought. Christopher Slade saw and understood more than his eleven-year-old mind could yet articulate. She said softly, "You want to give Max his life back."

He nodded, his eyes shining. "Yeah. That's it. He's done so much for my brothers and me."

"It was his choice, Christopher. I can't imagine he'd want you to feel this burden. To be frank with you,

Max has known where to find me these past four years. If he'd wanted to, he could have gotten in touch.''

"He wouldn't do that."

"I know."

"It's not why you think. He just—he couldn't—" He broke off again, unable to put into words what he so desperately felt he knew. "You know him. You know how he is."

"No, Christopher. I really don't know him. Maybe that's the whole point."

"But I— You can't—" He screwed up his face, turning red. "Oh, never mind." Then he abruptly shot down a narrow path that intersected with the one they were on.

Calley, suddenly feeling jet lagged and dehydrated from the dry Western air, followed at a slower pace. She hoped she hadn't blown it with Christopher. But Max happier with her? Not likely. Even at their best, they'd been far from an ideal couple. Too many sparks, too much fire, too much heat. If he hadn't trotted off to parts unknown, they would have burned each other out.

No, she thought, Christopher was just projecting his own preadolescent confusion onto his older brother and guardian.

As she came to the back of the sprawling Slade house, Calley took a quick, furtive look around for Lucky. She wasn't convinced he was a harmless bird, but he didn't seem to be around. Perhaps off playing Frisbee with Wynne or Timothy or one of the hands, something she still had to see for herself before she'd believe it. Max Slade wasn't above telling her a tall tale just to show her how out of place she was. But he didn't need further proof of her gullibility. Her presence in Wyoming was proof enough.

She hesitated a few moments, studying the house, shaded with oak and evergreen, in as pretty a setting as she'd ever seen. It was perhaps seventy-five years old, painted dark brown, surrounded by shrubs and a prosaic yard. Calley could picture an herb garden just outside the kitchen door, climbing roses and perennial gardens. New Yorker that she was, she could appreciate gardens. There was a huge wooden swing set, complete with a climbing rope and trapeze and a platform covered by a bright orange tarp.

If someone had told her two weeks ago she would find Max Slade within five miles of a swing set, she would have laughed herself silly.

Maybe Christopher was just trying to reconcile the Max he knew with the one she'd known. Maybe she was doing the same. The Max of four years ago had loved city life and was in no hurry for kids, and he'd exhibited no interest in ranches or horses or cowboy hats. They'd had fun together, walking through Central Park, taking in museums, discovering new restaurants. But had she really known him? She hadn't even realized he had brothers, never mind that they were so young that in the event of their parents' death he'd become their legal guardian.

Well, it didn't matter if she'd really known Max Slade four years ago or not. He did not belong in her life.

And she was quite confident that whoever he was, the Max Slade who'd kissed her that morning regretted it.

Jimmy Baxter was pulling together dinner in the large, sunny kitchen. He grunted at Calley in what passed for a greeting. The Slade household seemed to operate on a loose set of ground rules, with everyone looking after everyone else. Six-year-old Wynne might *appear* to be on his own, but he never went unsupervised. Calley had noted that Christopher, although the eldest, wasn't expected to look after his younger brother unless it was clearly spelled out. He was free to be a kid himself.

If, she thought, he would let himself.

She found Timothy and Wynne in the large front room, banging on the old upright piano. She gritted her teeth at the racket. "You boys ever have piano lessons?"

Wynne looked at her as if he'd never heard of such a thing. Timothy shook his head. Calley sighed. Their "playing" would give her a headache in another thirty seconds. She had them make room for her on the bench. Wynne complained that he was half off and climbed up on her lap as if it came naturally to him. He was no lightweight, and he smelled like dirt and sweat. Kid smells, she told herself.

It had been ages since she'd played. She didn't have a piano in her apartment in New York. What did she remember? A couple of études and sonatas. They would go over big. What might these rascals know that she also knew?

"You boys ever see *The Sound of Music?*"

Wynne nodded eagerly. Timothy said, "Yep. Max hates it, though."

He would, Calley thought. Judiciously, however, she kept her mouth shut. Taking a moment to focus, she adjusted Wynne on her lap so that she could get her arms around him, then started to play.

She made a few mistakes and hesitated a couple of times, and once nearly dumped Wynne off her lap, but all in all she thought she did a respectable version of "Do-re-mi."

When she finished, Wynne said, "Wow, awesome."

"Wicked," Timothy said.

Calley laughed. "I'll take those as compliments."

Wynne slid off her lap, and Calley turned around on the wooden piano bench, only to find Max standing just inside the front door. She inhaled at the sight of him. She hoped Timothy, still beside her, didn't notice. She hoped *Max* didn't notice. He looked hard edged and exhausted, the humor and near-charm of this morning gone. His slate eyes penetrated her with an intensity she couldn't define. She had no idea if he were pleased to find her playing piano with his little brothers, annoyed, neutral, or even if he'd realized that was what she'd been doing. He was completely unreadable.

"Dinner's ready," he said. He glanced at his brothers. "You boys wash up."

Timothy and Wynne immediately scooted up the stairs.

Calley got to her feet. "Well, hello to you, too."

Max's gaze dropped back to her. "Jimmy's waiting."

He turned and headed for the kitchen. Calley scowled. Two weeks. Heck, she'd sure made *her* deal with the devil.

But she wasn't going to let Max Slade scare her off. No way. She would not be intimidated or put off by his deliberate surliness. If he wanted her gone, he could kick her out.

It was, she thought, a distinct possibility.

By her third evening at Black Creek Ranch, Max still hadn't kicked her out. He hadn't even hinted he wanted her to leave. He had simply, it seemed, done his level best to pretend she wasn't there. He would absent himself from her company at every opportunity.

It was, Calley supposed, easier that way for them both.

A magnificent sunset of reds and oranges and vibrant lavenders drew her outside after a barbecue of sorts. Dinners at the Slade household tended to be substantial but uncomplicated. Tonight Jimmy and Max had thrown chicken and corn on the cob on the grill while the boys played Frisbee with Lucky. The idiotic bird really could catch a Frisbee. He even seemed peeved when the boys switched to baseball. They'd pressed Calley into pitching. She'd tried to pretend she didn't feel Max's gaze on her, and hoped the boys didn't notice either of them. She wasn't sure what Jimmy Baxter noticed, not that it mattered. He was decidedly the type to keep his mouth shut and mind his own business.

With the sun setting and the boys inside watching a video, Calley walked with one of the big dogs down to the wide, rolling meadow that paralleled Black Creek. Horses, mostly Appaloosa, grazed among the grass and wildflowers. She leaned against the fence, its design the picturesque "buck and rail" common to the region. She breathed in the clean air.

"Pretty, isn't it?"

Max came up beside her, his slate eyes taking in the sunset from beneath the brim of his dusty hat. She briefly wondered if such a hat would have looked right on him when he was in New York. Now it looked almost a part of him.

"Yes," she said. "Very pretty."

"I used to like watching the sunset from the roof of my building in New York. There was a deck up there."

"I remember," she said.

He acknowledged her words with a small nod, still not looking at her. They'd had wine together on his rooftop deck. Morning coffee. Long talks. They'd imagined their future together. Or at least, Calley thought, she had. She no longer knew what Max really had been thinking—what he'd wanted, what he'd feared—during their months together.

"It was relaxing after a wild day on Wall Street," he went on, pensive. "I felt as if I were above the fray, removed from it at least for a while. It restored my spirits."

"You never seemed too troubled by life in New York."

"Not when I knew you, no."

His words were delivered without emotion, but Calley felt a warm shiver run up her spine as she remembered what she and Max Slade had meant to each other in those days.

He continued to stare out at the sunset. "Sometimes I'd think about being back here, but not often."

"Then you'd been here before the boys' parents were killed?"

He turned toward her, shadows shifting over his face. "What do you mean?"

"Well, so far, I've gathered that you and the boys have the same father, and their mother was his second wife and much younger than he. I don't know, I guess I've assumed your parents were divorced, and your father always dreamed of living in Wyoming and came out here after the divorce and remarried."

"For a financial type, Calley, you've got a vivid imagination."

"So I'm wrong?"

"Not entirely. My parents were divorced. My mother lives in San Francisco."

"Yes, I remember you mentioning that when we were going together. That's where you grew up, right? San Francisco?"

He shook his head. "No. I grew up here."

"*Here?* You mean you're from the wilderness? I never had a clue. You never said—"

"My parents divorced when I was fifteen." He spoke matter-of-factly, without emotion. "My mother lived in Jackson until I graduated high school. Then she took off, and so did I."

Calley winced. She'd known nothing about this man when they were together. *Nothing.*

She still didn't. Four years ago, she'd fallen in love with a mirage. She'd fallen for the man she'd wanted Max Slade to be, not the man he was.

"Surprised?" he asked, amused.

"Well, I'd always figured—I guess I thought—"

"You assumed I was a city boy, born and raised."

"Yes, I suppose I did." She tried to keep her focus on the sunset that seemed to envelop them, rather than on the hardened man beside her. "I never would have said you'd grown up on a Wyoming ranch. I can't believe you never mentioned it when we were going together."

He shrugged. "I guess it just never came up."

"Did you hate growing up here?"

"No, I didn't hate it. It wasn't easy, but it had its moments, good and bad. My parents weren't happy together for a long time, and the isolated life out here didn't help matters. It's not as bad as it used to be. The area's grown."

He paused a moment, and Calley thought she could see a glimpse of the boy he'd been, lonely, torn, driven. Then the mask dropped, and the hardness of the man he'd become closed in.

"Things change, I guess," he said.

"This was your father's ranch?" Calley asked.

"It's been in the Slade family almost a hundred years. We've always bred and boarded horses. My great-grandfather earned a lot of money in the silver mines, and this was what he wanted, a Wyoming ranch, land as far as the eye could see. My father loved it here."

"Did he approve of your moving to New York?"

"It didn't much matter whether he approved or not. I went."

"Max—"

"I mean to see that my brothers have a better life than I did. My father wasn't an easy man, but he was happier with Lissa, less driven and difficult, less controlling—more content inside his own skin, if that makes any sense. If he'd lived, I think he'd have been a good father to the boys."

Unfortunately, he hadn't lived. "What about their mother?"

"Lissa seemed happy with my father, despite the disparity in their ages. She wasn't that much older than me. We got along all right. She loved the ranch."

"She was from Wyoming?"

He smiled. "California."

A breeze stirred, carrying with it the smell of evergreen and wildflowers. Calley could hear the horses making noises, moving about. She was a long, long way from her life in New York. "So when she and your father were killed, you decided to come back here."

Max didn't answer at once. As he stared out at the same view she did, she wondered what he was seeing. The same beautiful sunset, or childhood memories charged with conflict, longing, disappointment?

Finally, he said, "I couldn't justify uprooting the boys. This was their home. They needed to be here, and so did I."

"I can see how Christopher might be confused about what happened to us." She turned around and leaned back against the fence, looking out across the rolling meadow toward the house. Dorothy beamed to Oz, all right. She'd never felt so out of place, so far from home. "I didn't go out of my way to impeach your character, but I've assured him the accident just gave you an excuse to hit the trail. You'd have found another way without it. Either that, or I'd have come to my senses and dumped you myself."

Max drew away from the fence, studying her through half-closed eyes. Calley was surprised at how unnerving she found his scrutiny. She made herself focus on the quiet sounds of the evening.

"You're still angry," he said finally.

"I am not." She snorted. "What an ego. I'm not some pitiful woman who's been nursing her resentment of some jerk ex-boyfriend. So you can forget that one. Seeing you again has just gotten me in touch with how I felt when it finally dawned on me that you'd picked up stakes and hit the road without so much as spitting in my eye.'' Though Calley knew she wasn't being completely honest, she needed to save face, and to shield her lingering pain from Max's probing gaze.

"Calley, I never wanted to hurt you."

"Water over the dam, Max. In hindsight, I'm glad you did what you did. I learned a lot about myself, men and you in particular. If we'd stayed together, who knows? I could have ended up trying to push you off the Empire State Building. We just weren't meant for each other."

He continued studying her, his expression suggesting she might as well have been talking to herself. "You were hurt, Calley. It's never been easy for you to admit your softer side. You like to think you can brazen your way through anything."

"Max, lest you forget, I *did* brazen my way through losing you."

"I should have called."

His tone remained quiet, serious, but something shone in his eyes that she couldn't identify—maybe didn't *want* to identify. Or she was just imagining it because of the hat. She would have to get herself a cowboy hat. Then Max could try to figure out things that came into *her* eyes.

He should have called. Right. Well, pal, she thought, you're four years late.

She started back toward the house. She didn't want to hear about what Max Slade should have done four years ago.

"I started several letters to you," he said behind her.

She stopped, but didn't turn around.

"I kept them. They're stuck in a trunk in a storage room. I think they're what led Christopher to you. I never finished them. I couldn't."

She inhaled, taking in the dry, clean air, trying not to read into Max's soft voice emotions that weren't there. He was setting the record straight. Nothing more.

"I was overwhelmed, Calley. My father was dead. Lissa was dead. My little brothers were orphans. In my own mind, I couldn't justify overwhelming you, too. I didn't want you to feel the same despair I was feeling. At the time, I thought I was sparing you, but now I realize I was just sparing myself. Deep down, I think I was hoping if you continued your life in New York without me, without knowing what had happened to me, a part of me would be untouched by the tragedy of Lissa's and my father's deaths."

Calley listened without interruption, but still made no response. What could she say? How could she compare the pain she'd felt when he'd abandoned her without a word to the pain he'd felt over two deaths? It wasn't a contest, she knew. But she still didn't know what to say.

"I was wrong, Calley."

"Max."

He didn't seem to hear her. "I know there's no excuse for what I did. But I couldn't put you into the position of having to choose between the life you wanted and deserved in New York and a life out here with me and three little kids.''

She whipped around, not expecting him to be so close. She nearly barreled into his chest, stopping herself just in time. "So you let me hate you instead."

"Yes."

"Mission accomplished. I've gotten comfortable disliking you, Max Slade. I wouldn't forget that if I were you." Her voice was low and intense, the anger and hurt and loss—the horrible confusion—she'd felt four years ago fresh again. "You can trust me not to undermine your relationship with your brothers while I'm here. I'm not staying so they can end up disliking you. I just want them to realize they went to a lot of trouble to get me here for nothing."

"They're not your responsibility."

"I know that. But I'm responsible for the consequences of my own choices and actions. I fell for their story, and now I'm here."

"Whatever goes on between us, I won't have those boys hurt."

She swallowed. She could feel his intensity, his determination to protect his younger brothers and meet his responsibilities as their guardian. But his determination was more than a question of duty. She could also feel his love for Christopher, Timothy and Wynne Slade.

"I couldn't agree more," she said. "But nothing's going to go on between us. You waltzed out of my life four years ago, Max. You can rationalize now it was because of grief and shock and wanting to spare me a difficult choice. But I believe you'd have found another reason if you'd had to. We just weren't meant for each other. Your brothers will see that before too long."

She whipped back around, the sun setting fast now, darkness gathering around them.

After a moment, Max said behind her, "Will *you* see it?" he asked softly.

She pretended not to hear him. Arguing with his sizable male ego would get her absolutely nowhere. So what if the basic physical attraction she'd had for him four years ago was still intact? So what if he'd abandoned her for noble reasons? So what if he wasn't living the life she'd imagined him living, filled with fancy restaurants and fast cars and beautiful women?

So what? she thought, marching up toward the house.

They hadn't belonged together four years ago. They didn't belong together now. Max Slade could go ahead and think what he wanted to think. He would know she was long and well over him when she boarded her plane and headed home to New York.

# 5

The woman had to go.

Max stumbled to the coffeepot at five in the morning. Jimmy Baxter was the only one up, doing his list for his weekly trip to town. He eyed Max from his post at the long, scarred counter. "Rough night?"

Max ran one hand over his morning beard and just glowered as he filled his mug. He'd awakened twice during the night thinking—dreaming—that Calley was in bed next to him. Not good. Scary as hell, in fact, considering she was a stubborn woman and no doubt meant to stay her full two weeks in Wyoming. Determined to prove there was nothing between the two of them, she was.

Just as well she hadn't been privy to his dreams.

But he wasn't about to explain his complicated feelings toward Calley Hastings to Jimmy. He didn't understand them himself. On the one hand, he wanted to put her on the next plane east. Hell, the next plane anywhere.

On the other hand, he couldn't stop thinking about them finishing what they'd started the other day in the guest room.

He took just one sip of coffee before he started for the back door. "I've got a lot of work to do," he said, knowing it sounded more like a growl. "Be down in the lower pasture most of the day. You and the boys can find me there if you need me. I won't be back for lunch."

Jimmy glanced up from his grocery list. "You're just making up work so you won't have to hang around here. Running isn't going to help, you know."

"I'm working, not running."

The old man shrugged his lean shoulders. Even with his bad leg, he wasn't to be underestimated. And Jimmy Baxter *always* spoke his mind. "You ain't got nothing going on down there somebody else can't do."

Max wrenched open the back door. He knew Jimmy was right. He liked to spend as much time as possible with the boys. They tried to have lunch together whenever possible, and they were always welcome to join him out on the ranch, provided conditions were safe for them.

But today, Max knew, he needed to be alone.

Before he could make good his escape, Calley materialized in the kitchen. Max hadn't heard her walking up the hall from the guest room, and her appearance took him by surprise. She had on jeans and her Knicks sweatshirt. No shoes. No socks. Her hair was tousled, and her eyes looked bleary behind the lenses of her glasses.

She yawned. "What was that noise?"

Max frowned. "What noise?"

"You didn't hear it? Sounded like all the beasts of hell coming after me."

Mystified, Max turned to Jimmy, who looked thoughtful a moment, then said, "Must be that barn owl. He usually isn't up and about this close to dawn. He's a real night fellow. Took up residence in the stable this spring. Don't often get barn owls this far north."

Calley was unimpressed. "Well, whatever it was gave me the willies. Look here." She pushed up one sleeve of her sweatshirt. "Goose bumps."

Jimmy shrugged. "Barn owls have a hell of a screech." He glanced at Max, his dark eyes clearly communicating a deep perplexity with city folk. An owl giving someone goose bumps? It was beyond the realm of Jimmy Baxter's considerable experience. He turned his attention back to his houseguest. "The fellow you heard'd swoop down and tear a mouse or even a cat to shreds, but he wouldn't hurt a big ol' gal like you."

Max suppressed a grin. Calley made a face and retreated down the hall, muttering about the damned woods, needing a little concrete underfoot and, no thanks, she didn't want to see a mouse ripped apart.

"I say something?" Jimmy asked.

Max laughed. "She's just not used to the country."

"Well, I don't think it was any barn owl scared the wits out of her."

"Don't hold supper for me," Max called, ignoring the last, knowing comment, and went through the door, out into the cool, dry morning air.

Around noontime, when he was sweating and exhausted and nowhere near to having worked Calley Hastings out of his system, Max spotted two horses coming over the rise. Christopher was on one, no surprise. But Calley was on the other, a big, gentle Appaloosa named Stubbs. She sat up high and stiff in the saddle. Anyone seeing her would have to guess she'd never been on a horse before.

Probably she hadn't, Max thought. However smart and experienced she was with money, Calley Hastings was neither with four-legged animals.

Christopher had been riding, if not alone, since before he could walk and was perfectly at ease on a horse, although Max had no illusions the eldest of Ernest and Lissa Slade's children would stay on the ranch or even in Wyoming as an adult. Max had vowed never to put that kind of pressure on any of his brothers. He would sell the ranch first.

"Jimmy had us bring you lunch," Christopher said, moving closer.

Calley frowned, hanging on tight to the reins. "Lunch? Who said anything about bringing Max lunch? I wasn't consulted. You drag me out into the wilds on some horse and practically give me a heart attack splashing through that stream—" She sputtered, Max noting, however, that she had managed her tirade without moving in the saddle. As rigid as she was, if she fell, she would hurt herself for sure. "I swear, I never want to hear you ranch types muttering about New York being unsafe.''

Christopher had turned around in his saddle, staring at her in bewilderment. Max grinned, expecting his brother was getting his first real taste of just how unsuited the woman he'd lured from New York was to life in Wyoming. Without commenting, Christopher dismounted, agile and unselfconscious, and got out the pack Jimmy had put together, devious old man that he was. Max had done without lunch before. It was no big deal. Usually he would mooch something off one of the hands, enough to tide him over until he got back to the house. Jimmy had never before seen fit to make sure he was fed. Either he'd wanted to get Christopher out from underfoot, or Calley, or both.

She still hadn't moved a muscle.

Max walked over to her. She had on a dirty white felt hat that must have been one of Jimmy's because it wasn't his, and it wasn't one of the boys'. It served to keep the sun off her face, but did nothing for her appearance. Her glasses were about halfway down her nose, and she had a smudge of dirt on one porcelain cheek. Max saw that she hadn't loosened her grip on the reins.

"Scared?" he asked mildly, without arrogance.

It didn't matter. Calley wasn't about to admit to being scared. She scowled at him. He thought he saw her grit her teeth. "Annie Oakley I'm not. I don't know how to get off this thing."

Max suppressed a grin. The woman did hate to admit a weakness, but he'd always admired her determination. "Old Stubbs here will let you experiment if you want to figure it out for yourself. He'd never throw off a rider."

"Just tell me what to do. I'm very good at following instructions."

"Since when?"

Her blue eyes fell on him, as scathing as Calley Hastings got, which was saying a lot. "Entertained by my predicament, are you, Max Slade?"

He let loose his grin. "More by your reaction to your predicament than your predicament itself. You can't stand not knowing something I know."

"Christopher," she called, deliberately ignoring Max. "Christopher, come over here and tell me how to get off this beast."

But Christopher was already back on his. "Can't. I promised Jimmy I'd come straight back. He's taking me to town with him." He got his horse moving. "Don't worry. Max'll show you."

"I've been plotted against," Calley muttered as Christopher trotted off over the rise.

Max laughed. "We both have."

Barely turning in the saddle and certainly not loosening her grip on the reins, she looked longingly back in the direction of the house, well out of view. "I could go on back myself—"

"You remember the way?"

"I think so. How hard could it be?"

"Real hard if you take a wrong turn."

She sighed, looking back at him. "This stinks."

"Besides," Max said, trying not to sound as amused as he was, "your glasses would fall off before you got halfway home."

She scrunched up her nose as if to urge her glasses back up where they belonged. "Halfway home is Indiana."

"Calley." He gently touched her knee, not wanting to startle her; every muscle in her body had to be tensed. "Let me help you off this animal. It'll only take a second."

She made a face. "I never even liked the merry-go-round as a kid. Gave me the creeps. Probably someone like me invented the subway. You walk down the stairs, you pay your fare, you watch your purse. Easy. Civilized."

"Calley."

"Oh, all right. What do I do?"

"Ease your weight down onto your left foot, keeping it in the stirrup, and swing your right leg behind you. I'll hold the reins for you. You can hang on to the saddle horn with your left hand if you want, but try to keep your right hand free or you'll get all tangled up."

He took the reins, not that she had let go. He was trying to be considerate of her fears, even if she was reluctant to admit to them herself. But he wasn't worried. He had no intention of letting her fall, and Stubbs wouldn't throw her. Being out of control was what she hated.

"Stubbs here is a good horse," he said. "He won't throw you or take off with you just hanging on to the saddle."

Calley didn't look particularly encouraged. "Left foot in stirrup, right foot up over the back, left hand on saddle horn, right hand in thin air. Oh, sure. I might as well be five on the merry-go-round again. It was bad enough with a wooden horse."

"You want me to pull you off?"

"No!"

"Then you're going to have to get off on your own."

"All right. I'll do it. I've had my wisdom teeth out. I can get off a horse. But don't you dare do anything sudden."

She seemed to be muttering to herself more than to him, psyching herself to do the deed. She could be a very determined woman. Max suspected she was more afraid of embarrassing herself than of hurting herself. Calley Hastings definitely had her pride, something he'd known when he'd left her in New York, not giving her the chance to join him in Wyoming. Her pride might have compelled her to take on his grief, his new life. He hadn't wanted that.

He made a move toward her.

She shot him a glance. "Don't touch me unless I'm in danger of being trampled or cracking my head open."

"You want me to push up your glasses before you get started?"

"Do not touch me, Max."

It occurred to him she might not want anyone to touch her, to avoid being startled atop a horse. Then again, she just might not want *him* to touch her.

She took a deep breath, eased her weight down onto her left foot and leaned forward. For a brief moment, Max thought she might surprise him and actually pull this thing off on her first try. But as she started to swing her right leg up and back, the horse moved just a hair, nothing an experienced rider would even have noticed. Calley, however, wasn't an experienced rider. Lurching forward, overcompensating for the horse's movement, she grabbed hold of the saddle horn with both hands. It was a natural move for a beginner.

But she'd forgotten about her right leg. Its momentum had carried it partially over the saddle, but with her left foot still in the stirrup, there was nowhere for it to go.

She was all tangled up, in no real danger of harm, but in great danger of humiliation. "I hate horses," she muttered. "I really do."

"You want a hand?" Max asked laconically.

"Just tell me what to do."

He suspected she wasn't screaming bloody murder because she didn't want to spook the horse. Stubbs glanced behind him, as if wondering what all the fuss was about. "She's from the city," Max said in his soothing tone.

Calley scowled. "You're damned right I'm from the city. What do I do now?"

She'd slipped half off the saddle, left foot in the stirrup, right leg wandering, both hands hanging on to the horn as if she were in imminent danger of being trampled to death if she let go. If he didn't tell her what to do, Max had a feeling she would stay like that until she ran out of steam and slid off or Stubbs decided he'd had enough and bucked her off. Either way, she would be off the horse and on the ground.

Max still had hold of the reins. "Take your foot out of the stirrup and drop down to the ground. You're practically there already."

"Easy for you to say. You're not the one hanging off this damned horse." She shifted around, apparently struggling to remove her foot from the stirrup as she started sliding off the saddle. "I can't do it. I'm twisted around the wrong way or something."

"You're too low. You have to pull yourself up a little."

"The idea is to get *off* the horse, not back on it."

"Calley—"

"I wish your brothers were here. They'd see I belong in New York. I can't—how long is this horse going to stand here?"

"Long enough for you to get off his back, I reckon." Her hat came off, dark hair shining in the noontime sun. Max had a marvelous view of her behind. He did not, however, comment on it. "If you let go of the saddle horn, you'll be fine. Your body will do the natural thing."

She snorted. "It's too late for my body to do the natural thing."

Max let that one go without a rejoinder, several options for which came to mind. She was mad enough as it was. She started to let go of the horn, but grabbed hold of it again, fast, before she could see that she wasn't in as bad a mess as she thought.

"I'm hungry," he said.

"Max, when I get off this horse, I swear I'm going to—"

He sighed. Enough was enough. Very deliberately, he tugged hard on the reins, sending Stubbs forward a full step.

Calley cursed both horse and man. Max seized the moment, grabbing her by the middle and hauling her down to the ground. Her left foot had wedged into the stirrup tightly enough that he had to yank on her to pull it free. Not a happy woman, she cursed him some more.

When her foot was free, he tossed her onto the grass and scooped up her hat.

She sat up spitting and sputtering, hair flying. "I thought you said Stubbs wouldn't throw me."

Max grinned, handing her the hat. "*He* didn't."

She was breathing hard, shoving the hat onto her head, unmindful of her hair hanging down her forehead. Her smart eyes narrowed on him as she figured out what he'd done. "It's your fault. You made him throw me."

"He didn't throw you. He just moved forward."

"Because you made him."

"Like I said, I'm hungry."

She was, too, from the looks of her, not that she would admit it. "Well, don't let me come between you and lunch."

He had before, in New York. Suddenly, without warning, he remembered making love to Calley Hasting with the noon sun spilling over them. It seemed forever ago. As if another man had made love to Calley Hastings, not him. The memory almost paralyzed him. She didn't seem to notice. She tore open the pack. Jimmy had thrown in some cold fried chicken, pimento cheese, crackers, cucumber wedges, purple plums and boxed chocolate-chip cookies. A veritable feast. What had the old cowboy been thinking?

Naturally, the meal wasn't to Calley's satisfaction. "Fried chicken? I didn't think anybody ate fried chicken anymore, and what's that red stuff in the cheese? Pimento? I stopped eating cheese spreads a couple years ago. They're loaded with fat. I don't suppose these are low-fat crackers?"

"Not if Jimmy packed them."

"You don't always eat like this, do you?"

"I didn't plan to eat lunch at all today, unless I scrounged a piece of fruit from one of the hands." He noted the small throw blanket Jimmy had stuck in the pack and pulled it out, spreading it on the ground beneath the endless sky. It wasn't like a summer picnic on Long Island, but northeast Wyoming's raw-edged beauty seemed to suit Calley's mood. "I guess Jimmy means for this to be a special occasion."

"My second time on a horse. Some special occasion."

"First time. Merry-go-rounds don't count."

She shook her head at him. "I was on a real, live horse once in college. A rich friend took me riding out at her family's place in Connecticut. It was a lot more civilized than this. No offense."

"None taken. No one would ever mistake Black Creek Ranch for Connecticut."

"That's for sure."

Max grinned. Now that she was on terra firma, her natural cockiness was returning. "You must have managed to get off your Connecticut horse."

"Yes. I don't recall it being any big deal. But I wasn't worried about rattlesnakes or running wild through the countryside, and I didn't have you there to distract me."

He settled back on the blanket, in the swirling shade of an oak. He could feel his morning's work and his bad night in his muscles. "So I still distract you?"

"Not still." She bit into a chicken leg, its high fat content not so great a deterrent she wasn't going to eat it. "You distracted me in a totally different way when we were going together."

"How do I distract you now?"

"Well, I never know when you're going to kick a horse out from under me."

"For a brass-tacks financial type, Calley Hastings, you have a way with exaggeration. I didn't kick Stubbs out from under you. I just urged him forward. You needed a nudge."

"Did you or did you not deliberately dump me off that horse?"

"I did."

"Not sorry, are you?"

"Not in the least." How had he managed four years without Calley Hastings in his life? He leaned forward, feeling the cool shade on his face. "Let's say you still distract me, too."

"But in a different way."

He smiled. "No. Not in a different way at all."

She quickly dug into the pack, pretending she hadn't heard him. "I think I'll try some of Jimmy's pimento cheese."

"Go ahead. I'll just sit here a minute and be distracted."

Her eyes shot up to him. "You know, Max, it's not going to work. I'm not going to pack up and leave just because I distract you, in whatever way."

"Who says I want you to leave?"

"Jimmy Baxter."

Max gritted his teeth. That old cowboy needed to learn to mind his own business, not that he ever would. "I'm the one who gave you the choice of leaving or staying the whole two weeks."

"But you wish you hadn't. Jimmy says—"

"You should be listening to me, not Jimmy."

She ignored him, spreading pimento cheese on a cracker. "Jimmy says you're not sleeping well. You're not eating well. You're making up work to keep you out on the ranch. He says you want me out of here so you can get your life back to normal."

"Then why did I let you stay?"

"Because you didn't realize I'd have the kind of effect on you I'm having—according to Jimmy." She popped the pimento-cheese-covered cracker into her mouth. "This stuff's pretty good. I think I'll get the recipe. Anyway, I'm not saying Jimmy's right. I'd never accuse you of trying to run me off just because I kicked your male hormones into gear.''

''Calley—''

''The idea is for us to show your brothers we're not suited for each other. I suppose that can happen if you kick me out. Jimmy says you'd never tell them the real reason—''

''I'm telling Jimmy to stay away from you.''

She gave him a smug look. ''Admit it, Max. *You're* the one who's not over *me*. You didn't kiss me the other day to prove I still felt some kind of lustful spark for you. You did it because you felt a spark for me. You *wanted* to kiss me, Max.''

''I don't deny it.''

''And you still do, and that's why you're hiding out here and trying to provoke me into leaving early. You don't want to look like the bad guy to your brothers, so you'll do what you can to drive me out.''

Max stretched out his legs, eyeing her under the brim of his hat. ''Let me get this straight. I want you out of here because I want to kiss you?''

''Possibly more than kiss me.'' Her tone was brisk, businesslike. ''It's just libido, of course. We both know that. Nothing will come of it, physically or emotionally.''

''Calley.''

''What?''

''Quit thinking and eat your lunch before you get yourself into trouble.''

''I—''

But she looked at him and apparently thought better of arguing, and instead spread another cracker with pimento cheese. Max wondered if she realized she already was in trouble.

He knew he was.

# PLAY

## SILHOUETTE'S

# LUCKY HEARTS

# GAME

## AND YOU GET

★ **FREE BOOKS**

★ **A FREE GIFT**

★ **AND MUCH MORE**

TURN THE PAGE AND
DEAL YOURSELF IN →

# PLAY "LUCKY HEARTS" AND GET . . .

★ **Exciting Silhouette Yours Truly™ novels—FREE**

★ **PLUS a lovely Austrian Crystal Necklace—FREE**

# THEN CONTINUE YOUR LUCKY STREAK WITH A SWEETHEART OF A DEAL

1. Play Lucky Hearts as instructed on the opposite page.
2. Send back this card and you'll receive brand-new Silhouette Yours Truly™ novels. These books have a cover price of $3.50 each, but they are yours to keep absolutely free.
3. There's no catch. You're under no obligation to buy anything. We charge nothing — ZERO — for your first shipment. And you don't have to make any minimum number of purchases — not even one!
4. The fact is thousands of readers enjoy receiving books by mail from the Silhouette Reader Service. They like the convenience of home delivery…they like getting the best new novels month before they're available in stores…and they love our discount prices!
5. We hope that after receiving your free books you'll want to remain a subscriber. But the choice is yours — to continue or cancel, anytime at all! So why not take us up on our invitation, with no risk of any kind. You'll be glad you did!

NOT ACTUAL SIZE

*You'll look like a million dollars when you wear this lovely necklace! Its cobra-link chain is a generous 18" long, and the multi-faceted Austrian crystal sparkles like a diamond!*

## SILHOUETTE'S

*With a coin— scratch off the silver card and check below to see what we have for you.*

201 CIS A749 (II-SII - YRT-06/96)

**YES!** I have scratched off the silver card. Please send me all the free books and gift for which I qualify. I understand that I am under no obligation to purchase any books, as explained on the back and on the opposite page.

NAME

ADDRESS                                                      APT.

CITY                          STATE                    ZIP

**Twenty-one gets you 4 free books, and a free Austrian crystal necklace**

**Twenty gets you 4 free books**

**Nineteen gets you 3 free books**

**Eighteen gets you 2 free books**

Offer limited to one per household and not valid to current Silhouette Yours Truly™ subscribers. All orders subject to approval.

© 1990 HARLEQUIN ENTERPRISES LIMITED.

**PRINTED IN U.S.A**

## THE SILHOUETTE READER SERVICE™: HERE'S HOW IT WORKS

Accepting free books places you under no obligation to buy anything. You may keep the books and gift and return the shipping statement marked "cancel". If you do not cancel, about a month later we'll send you 4 additional novels, and bill you just $2.69 each plus 25¢ delivery and applicable sales tax, if any.* That's the complete price—and compared to cover prices of $3.50 each—quite a bargain! You may cancel at anytime, but if you choose to continue, every other month we'll send you 4 more books, which you may either purchase at the discount price…or return at our expense and cancel your subscription.
*Terms and prices subject to change without notice. Sales tax applicable in N.Y.

# 6

Calley was expounding on the virtues of New York bagels a couple of hours after Max had grabbed one of the hands, put her back on her horse and set the two of them on the trail back to the house. She'd gotten off old Stubbs just fine. She hadn't needed any help from a ranch hand who had a patch over one eye and reminded her of John Wayne in *True Grit*. He'd looked as if he would have no truck with some New Yorker who didn't know how to dismount a horse.

If nothing else, she was a quick learner.

Jimmy Baxter had returned from "town"—wherever that was—with groceries and odds and ends, and the boys had gathered in the kitchen for juice and frozen bagels. They thawed them in the microwave, tore them apart and browned them in the toaster. The two older boys put light cream cheese on theirs. Wynne had insisted on grape jelly.

It was all enough to make Calley gag.

At her urging, Jimmy had bought a tin of loose-leaf Earl Grey tea. He'd directed her to the pantry, where she'd unearthed a teapot that she now had steeping.

Miraculously, he'd also produced a small, dented strainer that fitted over a cup. Wynne and Timothy, and even Christopher, showed an interest in the entire process, the Slade household apparently devoid of tea drinkers.

The three boys watching closely, Calley poured a little of the tea into her china cup, which she'd retrieved from the dining room. Jimmy had warned her to wash it out first. Neither the china nor the dining room was used often.

The tea was the perfect strength. The boys munched on their bagels as she poured the tea through the strainer. She eyed the bagels dubiously. Cardboard probably tasted as good.

"Sometimes in the morning on my way to work," she said, "I'll stop off at a deli where they bake their own bagels. I get them warm out of the oven."

"With jelly?" Wynne asked.

"No, not with jelly. A light layer of cream cheese."

"I hate cream cheese," he said.

She had already discovered Wynne was remarkably forthright about his likes and dislikes. She liked a kid who spoke his mind. The two other boys munched on their bagels as she added a dollop of milk to her tea.

"How come you don't use a tea bag?" Timothy asked.

"I prefer loose leaf when I can get it, and when I have time. Tea bags are fine in a pinch."

"I hate tea," Wynne said.

Christopher finished the last of his bagel. "I want to go to New York sometime."

Calley remembered "Jill Baxter's" believable, wrenching desire to experience life beyond Wyoming. How much of that longing had been Christopher Slade's own? She smiled at him. "I'm sure you will."

"Max used to live in New York," Wynne said, squirming onto her lap. After a day playing outside, he smelled like sweat and dirt, and had to be the filthiest child alive. But she found, to her surprise, she didn't even have to repress an impulse to dump him off her lap.

Timothy nodded thoughtfully. "Dad said Max never wanted to come back to Wyoming. He liked New York. He'd have lived there forever if—"

"You don't know that."

Max spoke as he walked into the kitchen through the back door, his deep voice catching Calley off guard. He looked tall and dusty and tired, and utterly male. His presence immediately changed the mood of the offhand conversation she had going with his brothers. They looked caught, as if they'd strayed into forbidden territory. But Calley noticed no fear in their expressions, only respect. They weren't intimidated by their big brother.

His tone softened. "I don't know it, either. It's something none of us can know."

Wynne scooted off Calley's lap. She immediately felt ten degrees cooler. The kid seemed to radiate heat and energy. He ran up to Max. "Did you eat New York bagels?"

"Sometimes. Why?"

"Calley says they're the best."

She sipped her tea as nonchalantly as she could manage with Max Slade in the room. She saw no reason to apologize for her opinions. "They're better than frozen grocery-store bagels, for sure."

Max didn't respond. He went to the sink to wash his hands, and Calley watched him soap them up. It was enough to make her squirm. She didn't know why. She only hoped the boys weren't old enough to notice her reaction or attribute any significance to it if they did.

"I'm not much on bagels," Max said.

"Yes," Calley said, "I remember."

Christopher glanced at her as if he'd finally confirmed that she and Max really had known each other in New York and it hadn't all been a figment of his active imagination. The kid, Calley thought, missed nothing.

"I want to see the Empire State Building," Timothy put in. "Are you ever going to take us to New York, Max?"

"Maybe."

The man was in a taciturn mood, Calley decided. Was it fatigue? Too much Wyoming sun? Her?

So far as she could see, his little brothers paid no attention to his mood, refusing to let it dampen their spirits. Christopher started yammering about the Statue of Liberty, Ellis Island and the Museum of Natural History, but Wynne was stuck on bagels and Timothy on the Empire State Building. Max just continued to wash his hands, letting the boys go on. They seemed to believe he was listening. Maybe he was. Mesmerized by the almost sensual motion of his handwashing, Calley couldn't even guess what was on Max Slade's mind.

He turned from the sink, drying his hands with a flour-sack towel. "We'll worry about New York another day."

Wynne draped his stuffed puppy over one shoulder. "Calley says—"

"Calley knows New York," Max said. "I'll give her that."

Christopher, looking thoughtfully at his older half brother, suggested his brothers join him in departing from the kitchen. He promptly made good his exit. Timothy retreated to the living room to practice his piano lessons. Wynne, however, wasn't going anywhere.

Max took a seat at the table where Calley had given up any notion of having a cup of tea in peace and quiet. She refilled her cup. Wynne crawled up on Max's lap. Max hardly seemed to notice the extra weight, the dirt, the sweat. He frowned at Calley. "What's this I hear about piano lessons?"

She shrugged. "Oh, I'm just introducing Timothy to the keyboard. It's no big deal. He's really very interested."

"Can't accomplish much in two weeks."

"I don't intend to."

Wynne swung around, looking eagerly up at Max. "Can I take lessons, too?"

"Actually," Calley said, "you should wait until you can read. It'll be easier. Right now, you can mess around on an electronic keyboard or maybe get a recorder."

"Cool. Can I get a recorder, Max?" As if he knew what one was.

Max looked ready to growl. "New York, bagels, piano lessons, recorders. Anything else you've got these boys wanting?"

Wynne, either sensing a shift in mood or more likely just bored, wriggled off Max's lap and skipped off to join Timothy in the front room. Calley heard Jimmy barking at him to wash up before he touched anything. Wynne protested that his hands *were* clean.

Max had his searing slate eyes pinned on Calley. "It's not fair to let those boys get attached to you."

"What, I should be an ogre so they'll be glad to see me go?"

His expression didn't change. "The point is for them to see that we don't belong together. If they like you, they won't understand why I don't want to marry you."

Calley nearly spit out her tea. "*Marry* you? Who said anything about marriage? They just hauled me from New York so we could—I don't know—have some fun together. I never assumed they thought we'd end up *married*."

"Then you are naive."

"I never claimed to be an expert on kids. Your brothers hoodwinked me into coming here in the first place, so I have no confidence in my judgment where they're concerned. But marriage—" She scoffed. "They're little boys. What do they know about marriage? I'm sure that just because I'm nice to them they won't jump to the conclusion that I'm in love with you or that you ought to be in love with me. I mean, they can't possibly think like that."

"Of course they think like that. If they didn't, you wouldn't be here."

She set her cup on its matching saucer, her pleasure at having a nice afternoon tea vanishing under Max's scrutiny and dark mood. "So you want me to act like a jerk so they'll see why you dumped me four years ago. They won't blame you or themselves. It won't matter why you don't want me in your life now. They'll just be glad to see Calley the Jerk head back to New York."

He sighed with barely disguised impatience. "You don't have to act like a jerk. But you don't have to give piano lessons and talk about New York. Just keep to yourself and enjoy your stay."

"Pretend your brothers don't exist? Ignore them?"

"I didn't say that. Just don't let them become attached to you. Be distant. Pretend you're staying in a bed and breakfast on vacation and don't want to be bothered with kids." His eyes seemed to darken. "Which you don't."

"You don't know anything about what I do and don't want, Max Slade. And this isn't like any bed and breakfast I'd ever stay at."

"All right. Pretend it's a dude ranch."

"Me? At a dude ranch?"

"Calley—"

"Okay, okay. I can see I'm making you cranky."

Max said nothing, her light tone having no visible impact on his dark expression. She swallowed, suddenly aware of how damned sexy he looked all dressed up like a cowboy. He *was* a cowboy of sorts: born and raised on a Wyoming ranch and running it for the past four years. Who would have ever thought? Max Slade as Clint Eastwood? It would amuse his friends back in New York, if he had any left.

Then again, who would have ever thought she, Calley Hastings, would fall for a sob story by three preadolescent boys? People did have their surprises, she supposed.

Max leaned forward, his intensity not lessening one iota. He said in a deep, low voice, "I wouldn't call 'cranky' what you make me, Calley."

"Then what would you call it?"

Something gleamed in his eyes, and she caught her breath, realizing what a stupid question *that* had been. A sudden image of them in bed together assaulted her mind and senses. She could almost feel his mouth on her.

She managed, just barely, to eke out her next words. "Never mind. I withdraw the question."

Max shot to his feet. She wondered if he'd had any images assault him, but decided she would be a fool to ask. She didn't want to know. What good would it do anyway? There had never been any problem between them in bed and probably still wouldn't be, not that she had any intention of finding out.

"Just keep your distance," he said, and retreated to the front room.

Calley judiciously chose not to follow him.

The unearthly screech of the barn owl jolted Max awake well after midnight. He couldn't go back to sleep. The owl, he knew, wasn't the problem. Finally, he pulled on a pair of jeans and a flannel shirt and headed downstairs, aware of the other people asleep in the house: three boys, Jimmy Baxter and one woman from New York City.

Had the owl awakened his houseguest, too?

He crept past the closed guest-room door and into the kitchen. Night-lights he'd installed for the boys provided the only illumination. There were no street-lights out on Black Creek Ranch. He wondered if Calley had noticed.

The night drew him outside. The air was clear and still, cooler than he'd expected. Again came the screeching, eerie cry of the barn owl. It seemed very close, ghostlike. Max had no romantic illusions about owls; they were top-of-the-food-chain animals, pred-ators. He'd seen them rip apart tiny baby birds.

Down toward the stable, the silhouette of a female figure took him by surprise. It had to be Calley, of course—never mind that he wouldn't have expected her to venture out at night. She had her back to him. As he moved closer, he could see that her dark hair was tousled from sleep, or perhaps an attempt at sleep. She had on some kind of sweatshirt that was pulled down over a filmy ankle-length nightgown, its fabric drawn close to her legs. She was staring up at the sky.

Max wasn't sure if she'd heard him. He approached carefully so as not to startle her.

She spoke as he came up behind her, apparently very aware of his presence. "What an incredible sky," she said.

Max wasn't sure if the night sky really had captivated her, or if she were using it as an excuse to explain why she was outside before dawn. Being caught looking at stars wouldn't sit well with her urban self.

"I've never seen so many stars," she went on, still without looking at him. "No city lights to wash them out, no buildings to distract. Just stars. Do you know any of the constellations?"

"Some."

Turning around, she looked at him, her eyes luminous in the darkness. He thought she smiled slightly. He couldn't be sure. "Point some out," she said.

He moved closer to her. He could smell her hair and the baby powder on her skin. She must have bathed before bed. An image flashed of him applying powder to her stomach, her breasts. It must have been in another lifetime. How could he have left her otherwise? But he'd been a different person then, he reminded himself. Committed to his life in New York. Determined never to return to Wyoming to stay. Resolved to his father having started a new life and a new family, and to give all his love and attention to carry on the Slade ranching tradition. Then the phone call had come, and Max's life had changed. He had changed. There was no going back.

He pointed out the Big Dipper, which Calley claimed she knew, and Pegasus, Hercules, the Northern Cross. At first she didn't make out Cassiopeia, but applied her powers of concentration to the task, gazing up at the sky. Then she jumped, excited and pointed. "I see it!"

Max smiled. "It's fun when you start seeing the constellations. Makes the night sky come together a little."

"I can't remember ever seeing so many stars."

"One of the perks of living out here."

"Yes."

She seemed wide-awake. Max wondered if she'd slept at all. He and the boys had played cards before bed. Calley discreetly joined in only two games. Timothy and Christopher had caught her letting their little brother win, which they never did. She'd pointed out who was eleven and who was nine and who was just six, and maintained she'd only leveled the playing field. They hadn't bought it. Wynne, of course, had gloated, almost as obnoxious about winning as he was about losing. Calley had tried to give him tips on being a gracious winner, but he'd had none of it.

Max hadn't intervened. Calley Hastings and the boys would have to figure each other out for themselves. After she'd retreated to her room, Max had watched a video with the boys, then shooed them off to bed while he sat up reading. Concentrating was no easy task when he knew Calley was in the same house. When he went to the kitchen for a drink, he'd seen the light under her door. The boys were asleep. Jimmy was out for the evening. Max had only to knock on her door. Maybe she would let him in. Maybe she would tell him to go to hell. How would he know if he didn't do it?

But he hadn't. He'd taken his book and gone up to bed, frustrated and annoyed with himself.

Calley drifted into silence beside him. Finally, she said, "I can leave in the morning."

"Calley—"

"No, don't. I've been thinking about it." She turned sideways, facing him. Her face was cast in shadows, impossible to read. "We both know it's for the best."

He nodded. He knew. She was a complication the Slade household just didn't need. Four years ago, he'd made up his mind to go on without her, no matter the cost. What was the point in undoing what had been done? Never mind that her presence had reminded him how much he'd once loved Calley Hastings, how alive he felt around her, how very much he'd lost the day he'd packed up and left New York without her. But there was no going back. She knew that as well as he did.

"I'm sorry, Calley. If I'd known what the boys were up to, I'd have put a stop to it. Now you've given up two weeks' vacation. It won't be easy making new plans at this late date, and the money—"

"It's okay, Max. Playing Frisbee with a turkey and nearly getting bucked off some stinky horse have revived my appreciation for life and work in New York."

He managed a small smile. "Don't let Stubbs hear you say he stinks."

"*All* horses stink."

"Even Connecticut horses?"

She didn't smile, her mood pensive yet difficult to read. Was she glad to be going? Did she have any doubts? Was she acting for her own sake, the boys', even his?

"I've already made my reservation," she said. "There's a flight out in the morning, around ten. I caught Jimmy when he came in and asked him to drive me to the airport."

"He agreed?"

"More or less. He said I'd better have my mind made up because he wasn't going to put up with me changing it halfway to the airport. You know Jimmy. He's gruff and direct to a fault, but at least you know where you stand with him." Her eyes zeroed in on him. "Unlike you."

"I've tried to be straight with you, Calley."

She shrugged. "Maybe, but you've always been a hard man to figure. Not that I care to figure you out, you understand. Anyway, I assured Jimmy my mind was made up. He said he wouldn't hold me to my decision until we were off ranch property."

"If you changed your mind halfway to town, he'd put you on that plane anyway. You'd have to fly to New York and back again. He's like that. He's not the most spontaneous, flexible man around. I have the occasional go-round with him over the boys. But they understand him."

"I'm not changing my mind."

Max sighed. He wanted to look at the stars, feel Calley's shoulder brush against him. He didn't want to talk about what morning would bring. "Why are you leaving?"

"Because I don't belong here."

"That's a given."

"And because you have a point about the boys becoming attached to me," she added. "And me to them."

Her to them. Suddenly he could imagine it, where he'd never been able to before. Calley and kids in general—never mind three orphaned boys born and raised on a Wyoming ranch—were an incongruity—something that just didn't go together. Yet here he was, imagining her having an affinity for his younger brothers. Indeed, becoming attached to them.

It must be a lack of sleep, he told himself. Calley Hastings hadn't changed since he'd left her in New York four years ago. If anything, she was more urban, more suited to her fast-paced city life than before. When and if she became a mother, it wouldn't be to three orphaned boys on a Wyoming ranch. Max could let her leave because of them, but he couldn't let her stay because of them. If ever she chose to stay, it would have to be because of him, not his brothers.

He turned, abruptly starting back toward the house. Calley fell in beside him. He could hear her breathing. "I'm not going to ask you to stay," he said.

"I don't expect you to."

"But I'm not going to throw you out."

She nodded without comment.

All at once, without any warning, he stopped dead in his tracks. Calley nearly plowed into him. He touched her hair at her temple, sucking in his breath at the feel of her cool skin. She didn't pull back.

"I wish we could have ended things some other way," he said. "Some way that wouldn't have left either of us hurt, angry or wondering."

"So do I."

"I should have finished one of my letters to you, should have mailed it."

"Maybe I should have tried to find you, talked to your co-workers, trusted you enough to know something had to have happened for you to leave me high and dry. But what's done is done, Max. We both have to move on."

"I'll explain that to the boys. Obviously, they see more than I ever thought they did."

"I'm glad I came to Wyoming. Tell them that. I needed the answers I've gotten out here. A week ago, I'd have said I was well over you, Max Slade, but that's not true. Oh, it's not that I want to resume our relationship where we left off. I'm over you in that way. But you didn't exactly leave me open and trusting of men and new relationships. When I go back to New York—" She lifted her shoulders in an exaggerated shrug, then let them fall. "I don't know. Maybe things'll be better on that level."

Max forced himself to nod, but he couldn't imagine Calley Hastings with anyone but him. He didn't want to. "I hope so."

"You were in shock four years ago. I'm not excusing what you did. I don't like people making choices for me, 'sparing' me the burden. But I do understand a little better where you were coming from, and if it makes a difference, I do forgive you."

"It makes a difference."

"And I forgive myself," she added quietly.

"For what?"

"For hating you. For blaming myself. It was the easy way out. I can see that now. Life should be so simple as my view of what went wrong, you the bastard and me your unwitting victim. But life's not like that, is it?"

He shook his head. "No." He dropped his hand to his side, only some bizarre sense of nobility keeping him from kissing her. She'd made her decision. Let her get out of Wyoming cleanly, without him muddying up her thinking. "But I'm not sure you do understand what I was feeling four years ago."

"Max, you don't have to explain."

"I was afraid if I called you—if I'd left a message and you called me—I wouldn't have had the courage to do what I knew I had to do, which was to leave New York and come back here. I couldn't take that chance. I'm all these boys have. I *had* to be here. And I couldn't force you to make the same choice I had. It all seemed so logical at the time."

"Yes, I can see that now. Look, my anger with you hasn't been all bad. Part of me would like to hold on to it. It got me through some tough times. I could always say to myself you didn't abandon me because of me, but because you're a bastard. Who but a bastard wouldn't have left some kind of word? I envisioned you off in Chicago or L.A., off with other women—women I wouldn't like. Maybe I turned too distrusting, too leery of being hurt again, but I can see I needed to be more realistic about people and less naive. I've grown up a lot in the last four years."

She had, he realized. In many ways she *wasn't* the same woman he'd loved and left so abruptly, so cruelly, out of his own fear and need and sense of responsibility. "I'm glad you came," he said simply.

"Me, too." She grinned at him, her mood suddenly lightening. "At least I know I really don't belong in Wyoming. I belong in New York with my friends, my work, pizza delivery, dirty subways, museums, all of it."

It was true. She did. Max smiled back at her, wishing he didn't feel so damned conflicted about the decision she'd made. She had to go. Sooner or later, she had to go. "I understand."

She was silent a moment. "Good."

He touched one finger to her lower lip, then kissed her lightly, gently. "Be happy, Calley Hastings."

And he went inside before she could respond, before he could carry her off to bed and convince himself he wasn't still in love with Calley Hastings of New York, New York.

# 7

"I've changed my mind."

Jimmy Baxter shook his head as he steered his spotless old truck down a straight, narrow, beautiful Wyoming road. "Too late."

They were in the long, narrow valley of Jackson Hole, somewhere between Black Creek Ranch and the popular, picturesque village of Jackson. Mountains—*serious* mountains, Calley thought—loomed all around. A meadow of wildflowers spread out on the right side of the road, a stand of what she had learned were quaking aspen on the left. Gorgeous country, no question.

But Calley was preoccupied with the predicament she'd gotten herself into. Stay. Leave. Prove to the Slade boys she didn't belong with their big brother. Prove to *herself* she didn't belong with their big brother. She didn't know what to do.

"I'll rent a car if I have to."

"It's summer in Jackson Hole. You might not find a car to rent."

"Then I'll hitchhike."

The old cowboy glanced at her. "You know, you sounded just as determined last night, except it was about leaving."

"I *will* leave. Just not today."

He spit something out his window. The truck still rolled down the road at a speed well above the posted limit. Jimmy Baxter, she had discovered, lived life largely on his own terms. "Supposing I do turn around and you change your mind again?"

"I won't change my mind again."

He snorted, not believing her for even half a second. She'd squandered any credibility she had left with him by announcing she wanted to go back to Black Creek Ranch.

Calley raised her chin, insulted and a little embarrassed. "Normally, I'm very decisive."

"Yeah, I'll bet you're decisive as hell when it comes to money. Men, on the other hand—"

"My changing my mind has nothing to do with men."

He raised both bushy eyebrows, not saying a word. He didn't need to. His expression made his dubiousness quite plain.

She felt color rise in her cheeks. "It's true. Max and I— It's been four years. There's nothing between us. Nothing at all. That's why I've changed my mind. If there were something between us, I'd have to leave. But since there isn't, I can stay."

"That doesn't make sense."

"Sure it does. It's just a little convoluted. I've been working it through in my own mind. You see, if either of us still harbored romantic feelings toward the other—not that he ever really did toward me, although there were certainly other feelings. Well, you know what I mean."

Jimmy grunted. "Yeah. I know."

"Anyway, if that were the case, I'd have to leave."

He still didn't get it. "I can see your point if one of you felt that way and the other didn't. Things could get ugly, especially you both being so stubborn and bad tempered about that kind of thing. But if you both felt the same way—"

"All the more reason to leave." She decided not to touch the remark about being stubborn and bad tempered. What did Jimmy Baxter know about her?

He shook his head in confusion. "Now that's downright crazy."

"You're not following my logic."

"Logic? There's logic here?"

"Of course there is. You see, if Max and I did fall for each other again, there's no way we could stay together without destroying each other, and we both know it. But it's too complicated for the boys to understand, and there's no reason to confuse or hurt them. So I'd leave."

"How come you'd destroy each other?"

"He's a Wyoming rancher with three little boys to raise. I'm a New Yorker with a New York career and a New York life. Enough said."

Jimmy was silent a moment, his mouth twisted in thought. Finally, he sighed. "Nope. Still doesn't make sense. You're saying you're staying because you're convinced Max and you don't have a chance together?''

"Exactly."

"If you did, you'd leave for sure?"

She smiled. "See. It does make sense."

"If you call that sense— Well, I won't get insulting. That the only reason you're changing your mind? Because you figure you and Max don't have any romantic feelings toward each other?"

"No. I have another reason."

"Is it just as logical as this one?"

She shook her head. "It has nothing to do with logic."

"Then I don't want to hear it."

She'd had no intention of explaining herself to him. Lying awake at dawn, she'd realized that what Christopher, Timothy and Wynne's manipulation had been about was, simply, their brother Max. They wanted him to be happy. They wanted him to stop sacrificing his happiness for theirs, to see that he *deserved* to be happy.

And they deserved to see him happy.

Just not with her, of course. But with someone. Before she left Wyoming, Calley wanted Max to see that.

Jimmy put on the brake and swerved to the side of the road, doing a U-turn with one hand on the wheel and way too much gas.

"You're taking me back to the ranch?" Calley asked.

"Yep. No need wasting money on renting a car, and I'm not going to have your hitchhiking on my head." He brought the truck quickly back up to speed, driving with one hand. "Well. Now I owe Max twenty bucks."

"Twenty bucks? What for?"

The old cowboy grinned over at her. "He bet you'd change your mind before you got to town."

"On what grounds?"

"Opposite the ones you just gave me. They were about as logical as yours."

She frowned, thinking that one over, wondering if she should be incensed or confused.

Then she got it, and she was instantly so mad she could have leaped from the truck at seventy miles per hour and flown herself back to New York.

"That bastard! That arrogant, miserable—he thinks *I* still harbor romantic feelings toward *him?*"

Jimmy remained calm. "I don't remember him using the word 'romantic.'"

"That's it. Stop the truck. Turn around. Take me to the airport. I'm going back to New York. I can't possibly stay if Max Slade has such a high opinion of himself that he thinks I would—that I want—that I—"

She couldn't say it, not to a near stranger. Forget romance. Forget happiness and emotion and what kind of life she wanted to live. Max Slade believed she would change her mind about staying in Wyoming because she still lusted after his body. Period. No other reason.

Of course, she did harbor a certain physical attraction to him. She was *human,* for heaven's sake. But that had nothing to do with her changing her mind.

Not for all the sagebrush in Wyoming, she thought, would she go to bed with that man.

"I mean it, Jimmy." She spoke through clenched teeth, not liking the idea of Jimmy Baxter and Max Slade placing bets on her state of mind. She had tossed and turned and agonized, and those two had wagered twenty bucks on what she would do. Of all the nerve! Obviously, Jimmy had his own ideas about what was between her and Max, ideas she doubted she would like any better than Max's. "I want to go back to New York *today.*"

The old cowboy shook his head, adamant. "Too late, missy. We're going back to the ranch. One change of mind's all you're allowed."

Calley got to Max before he could collect his twenty dollars from Jimmy Baxter and crow a little about winning their bet. He was in the office down in the main stable. It was a double room that hadn't changed much since his grandfather's day, except for the addition of a computer, laser printer and fax machine. But the atmosphere, complete with old filing cabinets, shelves and two big oak desks, remained the same. Max had added his own oak captain's chair, an heirloom from his mother's side of the family. Oil paintings his grandmother had done of the ranch and of a couple of the horses graced what wall space there was. A window looked out on the lower pasture and Black Creek. He couldn't ask for a better view.

He'd been talking to several of the hands, but when Calley stormed in, they cleared out, grinning, making the obvious assumptions. Max hadn't even tried to explain her. Not many women turned up on the ranch to see him, and none like Calley Hastings. They'd already figured out she was from New York. It hadn't taken much figuring.

She was dressed for the city, black pants, crisp white shirt, silver earrings and just the right amount of makeup for flying.

She waited until she and Max were alone before bursting. "Of all the egotistical, self-centered men I have ever encountered, you, Max Slade, take grand prize. I cannot believe you think I changed my mind about leaving because I'm—because I've thought—" She sputtered, so mad she couldn't talk. Or maybe it was just embarrassment because he'd called a spade a spade and had said what he knew was on her mind. But Calley was a woman seldom at a loss for words, and seldom embarrassed. "I'll have you know I am not lusting after you."

Max tilted back in his chair, crossing his ankles up on his desk. The color was high in her cheeks, and tendrils of hair had fallen into her face, despite the barrette struggling to hold the rest of it back. Her intensely blue eyes were fixed on him behind her glasses. It was entirely possible that Jimmy, having lost their bet, had exaggerated Max's reasoning on why she would change her mind and stay in Wyoming.

Then again, perhaps not.

He regarded her with frank amusement. "So the thought of going to bed with me hasn't crossed your mind since you arrived in Wyoming?"

She sniffed. "I don't have to answer that. You're not entitled to know my private thoughts."

"Is that a yes?"

"It's neither a yes or a no. It's a none-of-your-business. If I answer one personal question—even to save my skin—you'll think of another to ask, and there'll be no end to it. I need to protect my privacy. Obviously, you have no sense of boundaries."

"When's the last time you had an intimate relationship with a man?"

"I beg your pardon?"

He swung his legs back down to the floor and rose. "Sex, Calley. When's the last time you had sex?"

"I swear, I'll *walk* to New York if I have to."

He came around the desk. "It hasn't been four years, has it?"

"I'll bet I can get to Jackson before sundown. I'll sleep at the airport if necessary."

"We'll conduct a test. I'll kiss you as best I know how, and if you don't respond, I'll take your word for it that you haven't thought about going to bed with me."

She shot him a look. She couldn't keep ignoring him, and she knew it. "That's a challenge, isn't it?"

"Yep."

"You'll keep your word?"

"Sure."

"I don't trust you."

"Of course you don't. No reason for you to. But I'll keep my word."

"If I don't agree, I suppose you'll consider yourself right by default."

He grinned. "Either way, Calley, if I kiss you or don't kiss you, I'll still know I'm right."

"I swear, Slade—"

"I kiss you or I don't. It's your choice."

"All right, fine." She inhaled, that New York financial mind of hers thinking over all the pros and cons, all the potential consequences. She wouldn't just let herself go. She wouldn't just do what she knew deep down she wanted to do. Finally, she exhaled. "Go ahead, Max. Kiss me. I assure you, I won't respond the way you think I will."

"It's going to be a proper kiss."

"I can handle it."

As if it were gum surgery. Max smiled, moving closer. She didn't back up even an inch. Once committed, Calley Hastings had never been one to back off from a challenge, even when it was clearly in her best interest to do so. It was one reason she'd thrived in New York's financial world. Smart, talented people without a backbone got eaten alive there. He'd seen it happen.

But Calley wasn't in New York. She was in Wyoming. She was on his turf, and she would be wise to remember it.

Max slipped his arms around her. She snuggled in close. In for a penny, in for a pound. That was Calley

Hastings. But her body gave her away. He could feel her tension, her anticipation. She wasn't at all sure she'd made the right choice, and it had nothing, he thought, to do with him. It was herself she was afraid of.

"Change your mind?" he asked, his mouth close to hers.

"No."

"You want me to kiss you?"

"To prove a point, yes. It's sort of a clinical test."

A clinical test. He would give her clinical.

He covered her mouth with his, drawing her against him. The taste of her took his breath away, but he didn't want to concentrate on his own reaction. He wanted to focus on hers. He wanted her to feel what he felt when he looked at her, touched her, thought about her, dreamed about her. He wanted her to acknowledge that being near him drove her nearly as mad as it did him. He wanted to *know* it did.

Not that they had a future together. They didn't. But what they'd had together four years ago wasn't dead, buried and forgotten. Maybe it had to get that way. But it wasn't there yet.

He deepened his kiss—and it *was* his kiss, not hers. She was letting him take the lead. Insisting. Her response, so far, was tentative. Polite, even. He drew her tight against him, so that every inch of her body was in contact with his.

He'd changed, he thought. He was harder than he had been four years ago, his muscles toughened by his work on the ranch. He had more scars, more calluses.

Let her feel the changes in him. Let her know that he wasn't the same man he'd been in New York.

Except in one way. He had the same driving hunger for her he'd had then. But let her feel that, too, he thought.

Finally, when he was on the verge of finding some hayloft and making love to her until dawn, he ended the kiss and stood back, studying her reaction.

She was trying hard not to give him one. Her glasses were crooked, her eyes sultry, her breathing not too steady. Swallowing visibly, she adjusted her shirt and straightened her glasses and, finally, cleared her throat.

"There. You see? No effect."

Max smiled. "Right."

She glared at him. "Don't give me that knowing look. You don't know anything. You tried a toe-curling kiss on me, and my toes didn't curl." Her hoarse voice forced a pause; she had to clear her throat again. "End of story. You failed, Max."

"Uh-huh."

"Admit it."

"Admit what?"

"That you failed. Your toes curled, but mine didn't."

He moved back around his desk, shaking his head. "I'm not the one who has to admit anything. You are, Calley. Don't tell me anything if you don't want, but at least don't lie to yourself. You know damned well that kiss got to you."

She started toward the door, in no mood to admit anything to him. If he told her she wore glasses, she would deny it. She tossed him a parting look. "I'm going to tell Jimmy he should get twenty dollars off you because he didn't lose any bet. I didn't change my mind because I was lusting after you."

"Then why did you?"

"As if there could be no other rational reason!" She snorted, but Max was betting it was just a cover for her curled toes. "As I explained to Jimmy, I'm staying precisely because I don't have any romantic feelings toward you."

Max dropped into his chair, unable to resist a grin. "Who said anything about romantic feelings?"

She slammed the door on her way out.

# 8

Wynne pounded on Calley's door, yelling as loud as any six-year-old could. "Come on out! Come on out!"

She groaned, shutting the book she'd been pretending to read. Wynne Slade was not a child to be ignored. What Slade was?

After Max's challenge kiss, she had retreated to her room, the only place she could be sure of her privacy. She needed to sort out what had gone awry in her mental state that she'd actually insisted on turning back when she was well clear of Black Creek Ranch. She should have pressed on to New York.

Instead, she'd come back, and she'd risen to Max's bait and let him kiss her.

It could be argued, she supposed, that she'd kissed him back. Well, what of it? For four years, she'd been haunted by dreams of kissing Max Slade again. Why not make the most of the opportunity? Why not kiss him back and prove to herself her dreams were just that. Dreams. Not reality.

Except reality had been even more alluring, even more unsettling than her dreams. The Max Slade of elusive memory didn't compare to the Max Slade of stark reality.

In short, he had not disappointed. She wanted him no less after their kiss than before.

But of course, *that* had nothing to do with romantic feelings. He had not engaged her heart. She had not engaged his.

Or so she kept telling herself as she'd given up on sorting anything out and had, in desperation, grabbed a book.

She was committed to staying. Whatever manner of insanity had gripped her, she wasn't going to give Max the satisfaction of seeing her leave. He would say it was because she still wanted him and was afraid to admit it. He would say it was because of the kiss. He would say it was because she was a coward.

"Calley," Wynne whined. "Come on out."

"Maybe I'm taking a nap."

"You're too old."

"Never try to win an argument with a Slade," she muttered, swinging out of bed.

Hiding in her room wasn't going to accomplish a thing. Max would put his spin on that, too. He would say she was just avoiding temptation or some such nonsense. He had his own way of looking at things.

She sighed at herself in the mirror. She still looked as if she'd just had her toes curled by a kiss, never mind that it had happened three hours ago. Max had not gone unaffected, either. She had eyes. She'd seen what their kiss had done to him.

That knowledge, however, was of no consolation whatsoever.

Wynne pounded on her door again.

"You keep that up," she called to him, "and you're going to knock it off its hinges."

"Lucky wants to play Frisbee. And Fred wants to meet you."

She paused, her sweatshirt half-on. She had yet to meet Fred. She had yet to learn who—or what—Fred was. In her current state of mind, she had no reason to trust that Fred was anything she wanted to encounter.

"Who says I want to meet Fred?"

"You'll like him. He doesn't bite."

"Does he slither?"

"Huh?"

"Never mind."

Kids, she thought. Not realizing she'd tried to make good her escape from Black Creek Ranch that morning, Wynne didn't hold a grudge. Christopher and Timothy, however, seemed to view her near-departure as some kind of betrayal, never mind their antics in getting her to Wyoming. They'd given her dirty looks when she'd fetched a pitcher of water to take to her room. She knew enough about preadolescents to recognize a dirty look when she saw one.

Max was their big brother and guardian, she thought. Let *him* explain.

Except she was the one who'd run out on them, leaving only a promise via Jimmy Baxter that she would send postcards of various Manhattan sights. Well, she thought defensively, what was she supposed to have done? She was used to being responsible for herself, period. She wasn't used to dealing with kids.

*"Calley!"*

"Don't whine," she said, tearing open the door. "I hate whining."

Wynne blinked at her. "What's whining?"

"You could get a Ph.D. in it, kiddo."

"What's a p-d-h?"

She sighed. "Never mind. Now, what about playing Frisbee with Lucky and meeting this Fred character can't wait?"

He lifted his shoulders and spread out his hands in a manner that was deliberately cute, no doubt designed to keep her from extracting answers he didn't have. He'd wanted her out of her room and in his presence, and he'd succeeded in his mission. Tactics were inconsequential.

"You do know how to get your way, Wynne, my friend." She patted him on his sweaty, dirty head. "But I guess if you can't have the world spin for you when you're six, you never can. We'll do Lucky first. I'm not meeting Fred until I have a better idea of what he is."

"Oh. Fred's a snake."

She'd feared as much. "I hate snakes."

Wynne giggled. "You hate *everything.*"

She smiled back at him. "That's why I live in New York."

Calley didn't know what had brought the older two Slade boys around. Either it was her rusty, pathetic Frisbee playing—the turkey caught better than she did—or it was her reaction to Fred.

Fred was a big snake, the biggest she'd seen outside of the Bronx Zoo.

"He's not poisonous," Timothy said, as if that fact should make more of a difference to her than it did.

Apparently, Fred lived in the area just behind the stables, in a hole in its old root foundation. The boys showed her the rock where he liked to sun himself. Calley duly noted its precise location. She would not sun herself on the same rock. Although they'd named him, Fred was—mercifully—not a pet.

"Max said we can't bring him in the house," Christopher explained as they all gathered around the foundation, where Fred, having been disturbed by three Slade boys and one non-Slade New Yorker, had retreated into his hole. The boys were disappointed. Calley was not.

She shuddered at the thought of a snake in the house. Give her a sink full of New York cockroaches any day over a snake. "I'm with Max on that one."

"Yeah," Wynne put in, "Jimmy says he'll cook Fred for supper if we bring him inside."

Timothy nodded. "He would, too. Jimmy likes snake."

Calley could feel her brow furrow as she considered the implications of Timothy's statement. "Are you saying Jimmy— He wouldn't—he doesn't—"

"Oh," Timothy said, "Jimmy loves snake. He says it's got to be the right kind of snake, or the meat's tough."

They were teasing her. They had to be. Then again, this was Wyoming. Who knew what old cowboys would eat? Calley tried not to overreact. "He hasn't cooked up a snake while I've been here, has he?"

"I don't know." Timothy looked at his older brother for help. "Has he, Christopher?"

"Hmm." He thought a moment. Calley forced herself to remember he was a child with a vivid imagination he was all too willing to put to ill use. "I don't know, that stuff he said was chicken the other night could've been snake."

Timothy shook his head. "Didn't taste like it."

"I know it. Have you ever had snake, Calley?"

"No. I have not."

"Some folks say it tastes like chicken, but I don't think so."

Calley's stomach lurched. "What does it taste like?"

Timothy and Christopher looked at each other, considering how to explain such basics to a New Yorker. Finally, Christopher shrugged. "Snake tastes like snake."

"How encouraging," she said.

"You'd like barbecued snake," Timothy put in. "Jimmy does the best barbecue sauce in the whole world, and it's really yummy on snake."

"I *love* barbecue," Wynne, not to be left out, interjected.

Calley made a face. "You boys see why I like New York?"

Christopher didn't answer. He turned to his brothers. "Come on, you two. Jimmy said we had to get back and help him."

"With anything in particular?" Calley asked. "I'd be happy to lend a hand, if I can."

The oldest of Max's three orphaned half brothers glanced around at her as he started back around the stable, grinning in a manner that would give women fits in the not-too-distant future. "We're having a picnic tonight."

"Yep," Timothy said. "Jimmy's fixing his barbecue sauce."

Wynne skipped up the path. "Yeah! Yippee! We're having snake for supper!"

If she'd been anywhere but the wilds of Wyoming, with anyone but Slade males, Calley would have assumed they were just pulling her leg. But she'd been on Black Creek Ranch long enough to know to assume nothing.

Barbecued snake for supper was not beyond the realm of possibility.

"What're you looking at?" Max asked as Calley peered around him to get a good look at the platter of marinated meat Jimmy had just brought out to the grill.

She didn't spare Max so much as a glance. "This is chicken, right?"

"I think so."

"You could tell if it wasn't, couldn't you?"

"If it wasn't chicken?"

She nodded.

Max laid several pieces on the hot charcoal grill. He hadn't seen her since their kiss in his office. Jimmy had said she went out with the boys, who weren't too happy with her for trying to sneak out on them. Max had not risen to her defense, but was sticking to his original plan. However long she stayed in Wyoming, Calley's relationship with Christopher, Timothy and Wynne was for them to sort out.

"Calley, why wouldn't it be chicken? What else could it be? It's obviously not beef—"

"It could be turkey," she said.

He grinned. "Not with Lucky around."

"Well, it could be anything, really. It's boneless, and the meat's pale." She chewed on one corner of her mouth, clearly dubious about dinner. "If Jimmy had a mind to, I suppose he could slip us snake meat and we'd never know it."

"I'd know it."

"How?"

"I've had snake."

She winced, moving away from the platter. "You mountain men."

"I didn't say I liked it."

"Do you?"

He shrugged. "It's okay if you're really hungry and that's all there is."

"What about Jimmy?"

"Oh, he's had snake lots of times, or claims he has. You never know when he gets going with his tales. I still sometimes can't tell truth from exaggeration, even outright fiction."

"Would he try to slip snake onto the barbecue?"

Max set down his barbecue fork and eyed her. For all the upheaval she'd endured that day—leaving, coming back, responding to his kiss challenge—she looked none too worse for wear. In fact, she looked ready to take on whatever Wyoming threw at her. She had her hair pulled back and her dirty borrowed white hat on, and she wore a blue chambray shirt with the sleeves rolled up, tan jean shorts and running shoes. He could have swept her up into his arms then and there, something he chose not to mention when she had snakes on her mind.

"Why would Jimmy slip snake onto the barbecue?" he asked, fearing he already knew the answer.

"Because he's a former cowboy and probably thinks snake's good eating. How would I know? And I'm not accusing him of anything. I'm just asking."

Before Max could devise an approach to get the truth out of her, Jimmy Baxter himself graced the scene, limping in from the kitchen with another platter. "Thought we'd throw some squash on the grill. I like it fried myself, but I guess it's better if we cut down on the fat. I brushed a little olive oil on it and sprinkled on some oregano, like you suggested, Calley. Guess it'll taste all right. I don't know.''

She was eyeing the squash, cut in lengthwise strips, as if it, too, might be snake. She was, Max thought, a woman spooked. He picked up his barbecue fork and flipped the chicken, already nicely browned on one side. "Jimmy, Calley here thinks you might try and hoodwink us into eating snake and making us think it was chicken.''

Jimmy set the squash next to the platter of meat. "Why would I do that? If I cook up some good snake, I'm not going to pass it off as chicken.''

"You'd tell us," she asked, looking somewhat encouraged.

"Sure. Max, you know I would. I've got no reason to slip anything past anybody. I cook up snake, you all'd know it, and you all'd eat it, too. Right, Max?''

"Yep, Jimmy, that's what you'd do. I remember the time you fed us fried grasshoppers. You didn't try to pass them off as anything else.''

"Well, it'd be hard, you know, with those little legs of theirs—''

"That's it," Calley muttered, "I'm sticking to cold cereal and toast. You ranch types aren't to be trusted with meals.''

Jimmy sniffed. "That's what's wrong with you New Yorkers. You don't know good food when you see it. You're spoiled. You get out on the range with not even a grocery store within a hundred miles, never mind a restaurant, and you work hard and get hungry, you won't be turning your nose up at fried grasshoppers or snake or anything else.''

Calley was not in the least intimidated by the old cowboy. ''I have no intention of *ever* being hundreds of miles from the nearest restaurant.''

''City folk,'' Jimmy grumbled, stalking back to his kitchen.

''Fried grasshoppers.'' Calley gave an exaggerated shudder. ''That's even worse than barbecued snake.''

Max laid some of the squash on the grill. ''Seems to me the boys have had their revenge on you.''

''On me? What'd I do?''

''You snuck out on them.''

She sighed, quickly glancing in their direction. ''I know I did. But Max, they can't think I'm staying forever.''

''You promised you'd stay the full two weeks—unless I kicked you out first, of course. You didn't. *And* you added insult to injury by not saying goodbye. Their sob story to get you here notwithstanding, they have a heightened sense of fair play.''

''We're not supposed to get attached to each other, remember? If this were a bed and breakfast and I were a paying guest, I wouldn't feel obligated to say goodbye to the owners' children.'' She was squinting in the pale early-evening light at Timothy and Wynne on the swing set, Christopher tossing his baseball high up into the air and catching it. ''Of course, this isn't a bed and breakfast, and I'm not a paying guest.''

Her tone was almost whimsical, as if she didn't quite know where she was, or who. Max suspected their kiss had confused her. But to suggest as much to her, he knew, would only annoy her. She would lash out at him because she herself was confused. He knew the feeling. But he would let Calley Hastings figure out for herself what impact coming to Wyoming, staying on Black Creek Ranch, would have on her... *if* she had any choice.

She turned to him abruptly, eyes narrowed. For a raw instant, Max had a feeling she'd read his mind. "Don't you go getting any weird ideas, Max Slade. I *will* leave at the end of my two weeks."

He smiled. "Of course. You belong in New York."

"That's right." One of the dogs came up to her, looking for a handout, sniffing her fingers. She patted him on the head. "Bet you don't like snake, either, do you, sport? You'd like Central Park, yes, you would. You could chase pigeons to your heart's content, wouldn't have to worry about wolves and coyotes, no elk to tempt you. Yeah, city life."

Max made a face. She was the stubbornest woman alive. Had to be. "What if you change your mind and decide to stay in Wyoming?"

She shot him a dubious look. "Then I appeal to your sense of honor and decency, Max."

He arched a brow, implying the question.

She gave him a not-so-innocent smile. "I'm talking about the honor and decency that brought you back to Wyoming from New York to raise your brothers, not the weasel in you that had you issuing that challenge in your office."

"Ah. You didn't react as if a weasel had kissed you."

"I will next time. Trust me."

He grinned at her, unable to resist. "There'll be a next time, Calley?"

"Not on your terms, I assure you. But one challenge begets another. When you least expect it, Max Slade, I'm going to nail your hide to the hardest oak tree out here." She cleared her throat, gently shoving the dog on his way. Thoughts of kissing him and nailing his hide to anything had clearly distracted and unsettled her, not that she would ever admit it. "I'm counting on you to put me on a plane regardless of what I say I want to do. Who knows what's in the air around here? I might lose my mind and decide to stay. Don't believe it. Put me on a plane and tell me to call when I've come to my senses."

He flipped the chicken and checked the squash, digesting her words. Finally, he gave her a sideways glance. "Don't trust yourself around us Slades, do you, Calley?"

"Nope. I don't trust you Slades around me."

Calley immersed herself in life on Black Creek Ranch.

The Slade boys, having had their revenge, forgave her for sneaking out on them and encouraged her to join them on their chores as a way of learning about ranch life. She had a feeling it was more a way of getting her to do their work for them. They were devious rascals, but she was on to them.

Each was assigned indoor and outdoor jobs appropriate to his age. Christopher, being eleven, did more with the horses. Timothy was in charge of the dogs. Wynne fed Lucky. They all took turns—and generally argued about whose it was—cleaning up after him, a free-roaming turkey not the neatest of animals. Since she was determined to do ranch life, Calley acquiesced to taking a turn at the nasty task herself, just to prove she was no squeamish New Yorker.

It was no treat. Lucky was big even for a turkey.

The boys also took turns at caring for the other small animals, and Jimmy kept them well-informed on what they were to do regarding housework, meal preparation and cleaning up after themselves. None, however, was overworked, despite complaints to the contrary.

Calley got along with Jimmy, provided she didn't "girlie" up his kitchen. She took that to mean he had low tolerance for her filling little china cream pitchers with wildflowers, her afternoon teas with the boys, her request for dried currants and cranberries to make her own scones.

She would soften him up by getting him to talk to her about horses and his days as a cowboy. From what he said and her own observations, she'd deduced that Black Creek was no struggling ranch and Max Slade no pauper. In fact, quite to the contrary. Jimmy Baxter himself had never ventured east of the Mississippi River. His opinion of New York was forged by tourists, the news and reruns of "Barney Miller." Calley had the feeling her ignorance of ranch life only confirmed his prejudices.

Not that she didn't have *her* ideas about the Wild West.

Max, of course, continued to be a problem.

He was polite and deliberately nonthreatening, which was all the more unsettling *because* it was so deliberate. It said he could change at a moment's notice. It said he might challenge her to another kiss. It said he knew she was watching his every move, reacting to him, *aware* of him.

It said he knew too damned much about her.

Friends of Max's from Jackson and a couple from California who boarded several horses at the ranch came on the weekend. Jimmy packed a lunch for the couple, and they set off for the day. The friends—John and Maura Parker—brought their two kids with them, a girl, ten, and a boy, eight. Maura was an architect, John a chef at one of Jackson's trendy restaurants. They gathered on the front porch for ice tea and lemonade while Jimmy, at his insistence, made dinner. Max, meanwhile, was down at the stables dealing with some horse matter. Calley didn't ask what. Her knowledge of horses remained blissfully limited.

With thunderclouds gathering on the horizon, the kids joined in a loud game of cards off to one end of the huge porch. The Parkers, obviously trying to figure out who Calley was and how she'd ended up on Black Creek Ranch, offered to show her around Jackson one day. Through a series of polite, if transparent, questions, they elicited basic background information about her, intrigued when they learned she was a financial adviser from New York. They suggested they knew people in the area, themselves included, who could use her skills. With the growth in Jackson Hole and Wyoming in general, such local talent wouldn't go underworked.

Calley said that was nice, but she was only in Wyoming for two weeks and intended to go back to New York and her Wall Street office.

An attractive woman in her late thirties, Maura Parker raised an eyebrow in interest. "Do you live in Manhattan?"

"The Upper West Side." Calley envisioned her apartment, its view of the street, its charm, its shortcomings, and smiled, nostalgic. "I have a neat little apartment. I love it."

John shuddered. "I could never live in the city again."

"You're from New York?"

"Oh, no. St. Louis. We moved out here after the kids were born."

"We just love it," his wife said.

"That's nice," Calley smiled, not defensively. "But I don't hate the city. I'm not saying I hate the woods, either, but— Well, folks in Wyoming should be glad some of us still like city life or they'd be overrun."

As their conversation continued, Calley still got the distinct impression the Parkers couldn't quite figure out who she was or what she was doing with Max Slade out on Black Creek Ranch.

So the Slade boys, having big ears and even bigger mouths, provided an explanation.

"She's Max's old girlfriend," Timothy blurted.

"Yeah," Wynne said, giggling.

John and Maura both glanced at Calley, not bothering to conceal their curiosity. Calley smiled, noncommittal. She had no intention of explaining her relationship with Max. She didn't understand it herself anymore. She shot the boys a warning look, but they were oblivious.

His two younger brothers pressed Christopher into telling the entire gory tale. About how he'd tracked her down through their computer networks and pretended to be a lonely widow with five kids, a dying grandmother and a ranch. Once he'd figured out Calley had no idea her ex-boyfriend was living out west or even what had happened to him since he'd vanished from New York—or why he'd left—he'd persuaded her to come to Wyoming.

Maura Parker clapped her hands together, delighted. "What clever matchmakers you boys are." She turned to Calley, apparently oblivious to any embarrassment she might be experiencing. "You must have been *mortified* when you saw Max."

Max, fortunately, was still nowhere in sight and not able to witness Calley's expression, which was not nearly as delighted as Maura Parker's. In spite of her discomfort, Calley liked the other woman immensely. She would take frankness any day over phony politeness. "I wouldn't say mortified. I'd say—" Well, what she'd been was enraged, outraged, suspicious and not happy at all, which the Parkers could figure out for themselves. "I'd say I was surprised to see him."

John Parker was grinning. "I'll bet. You don't look the type to fall for such an obvious sob story."

"It wasn't so obvious at the time." She kept her tone matter-of-fact, as if they were discussing an error in judgment of no consequence, not one that had put her on a ranch in the middle of nowhere with an ex-lover she hadn't seen or heard from in four years. The boys were watching her intently. She could have strung them up on the spot for blabbing. But she went on calmly, "Christopher's quite the writer. He's imaginative and clever. He was very convincing."

"Yes, but you must have had *some* idea it was a hoax—"

His wife laid a hand on her husband's knee. "Perhaps not. We weren't there."

He got the message. "No, of course not. Well. Max must've—hell, if one of *my* old girlfriends turned up out of the blue—"

"Darling," Maura Parker said, "you'd better stop while your head's still above water. If Calley doesn't drown you, I will."

At that moment, Max climbed up the steps to the front porch. He had on a denim shirt with the sleeves rolled up, and there was a hard look about him that seemed to have become a part of him. His eyes caught hers, just for an instant. He seemed to understand that she was on the hot seat regarding her presence in Wyoming, although his expression was remarkably without sympathy.

"The boys here were just telling us how they hood-winked Calley into coming west," John Parker said.

"Were they? Well, Calley and I hadn't seen each other in a while." He poured himself a glass of ice tea, remaining on his feet. He drank. Then he glanced at his friends. "Looks like the storm's pushing south. You all up for a game of volleyball before dinner?"

All five kids leaped to their feet before the adults could respond. They started yelling about who would be on whose team.

Max grinned. "Guess you'd better be."

The kids decided there would be two games. First, the Parkers against the Slades. Calley would have to play on the Slade team, they'd reasoned, since Max was the only adult and Wynne would get mad and quit before they could get a game in, a comment designed to get him to do just that, something Max darkly pointed out to Christopher and Timothy. The second game would be the adults against the kids. Timothy started to say the adults could have Wynne, but re-treated when Max shot him a silencing look, and in-stead, he slung one arm over his little brother's shoulder and promised to show him a few volleyball tips.

"I don't need any tips," Wynne said, Slade stub-born to the bitter end. "I already know how to play."

Max glanced at Calley as the Parkers and kids pounded off the front porch. "You mind being a Slade for a while?"

She swallowed, then shrugged. "It's just a game."

"That's what I keep telling my brothers." He started down the steps, looking less tired than he had when he'd come up them a few minutes earlier. "It hasn't sunk in yet. They're Slades, too."

"Meaning they hate to lose."

He grinned over his shoulder at her. "But they do love to win."

# 9

Max charged from the kitchen out into the rain. It was a warm, gentle rain, unlike the storm raging in him. What in hell was wrong with him? Why hadn't he let Calley Hastings spend that first night in the airport and catch the first plane out in the morning instead of taking her back to the ranch with him?

He remembered seeing her, standing amid her luggage, radiating her energetic charm, her impatience, her uneasiness with her Western surroundings. She'd fallen for a crazy sob story. She'd come to Wyoming. She was *there,* and he'd been unable to force himself to let her go. It was that simple. He could have taken her to the Parkers'. He could have left her to her own considerable devices.

But he'd taken her home to Black Creek Ranch, and now she had two days left before she returned to New York where she belonged.

He kept moving, unable to do anything else, even to think. Through an open window, he could hear Timothy practicing the piano in the living room. Calley had given him a couple more lessons, and he'd badgered Max to find him a regular teacher.

"But if Calley stays, she can teach me."

If Calley stayed...

Max squashed the thought before it could fully form. She couldn't stay. There was no point thinking about what would happen—what *could* happen—if she did.

Wynne had taken over the kitchen table to play a game of solitaire Calley had taught him. It was simple enough for a six-year-old to comprehend, and easy to win, which he liked. He would hoot and holler every time he did.

At the first sign of rain, Christopher had retreated to his bedroom to write poetry in a blank book Calley had bought him in Jackson. It had pictures of the solar system on the front. Max hadn't even realized Christopher liked to write poetry. He'd asked to read some of it, but Calley had glared at him as if he'd just embarrassed the kid. Max didn't get it. Later, Calley explained that an eleven-year-old boy needed privacy and space to explore his artistic inclinations without having his sensitivities trounced on by a hardcase older brother with no poetry in his soul.

Max hadn't been entirely sure what she was talking about. He figured the kid just had a crush on his sixth-grade history teacher and was getting it off his chest. Calley had groaned at his comment, saying she rested her case.

"You respect Christopher's imaginative nature," she'd said, "but you don't understand it."

His mind back on the present, Max noticed that the rain had soaked his hair, had nearly soaked through his denim shirt. He didn't care. Piano lessons, solitaire, poetry. Calley's impact on Black Creek Ranch would be felt for a long time. Even the damned turkey would feel her absence. He'd taken up waiting outside the kitchen door until she came outside and threw him the Frisbee.

Madness, Max thought.

He'd taken Calley to Jackson himself and showed her around, let her play tourist for a day. She'd poked in the trendy boutiques and galleries, bought herself her own cowboy hat, sat in the shade of the central town square. They'd eaten lunch at John Parker's restaurant and talked about things she wouldn't mind doing if she had more time in Wyoming, like river rafting and kayaking and hiking in the Grand Tetons, maybe even going for a long bike ride.

It had been an amiable day, as if they were a pair of old friends.

Which they weren't and never could be.

Max exploded into the main stable. He was tense and distracted, in a dangerous mood.

She had two days left in Wyoming. Just two days. He felt no relief. He couldn't begin to define what he did feel. In Jackson, he'd imagined Calley staying longer, staying forever. He'd imagined a future with her. It was as if he'd been sucked back four years, to the days before his father and Lissa had died, when he'd wanted nothing more than to spend his life with Calley Hastings.

But it wasn't to be.

He intended to keep his promise to her. If she took leave of her senses and tried to tell him she wanted to stay, he would put her on a plane back to New York. That was where she belonged. He knew it, and so did she.

She was in the kitchen now, arguing with Jimmy over what color to paint the kitchen that fall. As if it made any difference to her.

Max brushed dripping water from his face and took a deep breath, knowing nothing had changed in four years. Nothing.

He'd loved Calley Hastings then, and he did now. But she still didn't belong in Wyoming.

And he couldn't leave.

Calley saw the blood dripping from Max's arm even before the screen door banged shut behind him. He burst into the kitchen, his jaw clamped shut, his face contorted more in anger, it seemed to her, than pain. Blood soaked the upper left arm of his shirt along a tear in the sleeve.

Calley abandoned her paint chips and rushed to him, never mind that she well knew Max Slade could manage without her help. "What happened?"

"Snagged a nail." He snarled at her through clenched teeth, ripping off his shirt as he started for the sink. It was after dinner, a cool, dark evening. "I'm fine."

"You're bleeding all over the place."

"It'll mop up."

"Max—"

He eyed her darkly. "Jimmy and the boys left yet?"

She nodded. "Twenty minutes ago. They looked for you to say goodbye, but they couldn't find you—"

He didn't let her finish, instead slamming his right fist onto the counter and cursing a very blue streak. With the boys safely out of earshot, he could indulge himself. And he did.

"Feel better?" Calley asked mildly.

He glared at her. "Not particularly."

"Seems to me you're more annoyed than hurt. Must have cut yourself doing something stupid. Want me to have a look?"

"No."

He cast his shirt onto the floor. Blood dribbled down his arm all the way to his wrist bone, mingling with the dark hairs on his arm. The wound itself was jagged, about three inches long, deeper as it wound down toward his elbow. Calley grabbed a flour-sack towel from a drawer. In spite of Jimmy Baxter's territorial nature, she'd learned her way around the Slade kitchen.

"It looks worse than it is," Max said.

Her hands were shaking. "One would hope."

"Damned nail was sticking out where it shouldn't have been. Hurt like hell." His dark eyes focused on her. "What're you doing with that towel?"

"Wetting it."

She'd turned on the faucet, dampening the towel with cool water, trying to ignore how close he was standing to her. He smelled wet, earthy. She swallowed, squeezing the excess water from the towel.

"I can sponge off some of the blood and clean out the wound. Your tetanus shots are up-to-date, aren't they?"

"Calley—"

"No communicable diseases?"

He sighed. "None. I was tested last month for insurance purposes."

"Insurance, huh?"

He managed a grim smile. "I knew that'd get a gleam in your eye."

"More so than the sight of blood, I assure you."

She turned to him with the towel. The expanse of tanned, muscular chest took her breath away. Scars that hadn't been there four years ago marked his abdomen, his shoulders, as if to remind her his life had changed since New York. He'd changed. She had, too. She wasn't as trusting, not just of men and romance, but of herself.

"I'll be careful," she said.

"I'm not worried."

"Are you like a wounded bear when you're hurt?"

"Just do the deed, Calley."

Her hands steadier, she dabbed at the wound, which appeared to be free of debris. If everything else had changed in four years, she thought, her physical attraction to Max Slade hadn't. Coming to Wyoming had proved that much to her. If they saw each other when they were eighty, she would feel that same potent, irresistible pull to him. It was just one of the givens in her life. It didn't mean anything. It certainly wasn't something she had to *act* upon.

Never mind how much she wanted to.

She shook off the thought, trying to concentrate on the task at hand.

What made matters worse, she knew, was that in the past two weeks she'd also discovered a new, utterly unfathomable emotional attraction to him. It was different than what she'd felt for him in the past. He'd been cocky, optimistic, determined, driven. It wasn't that he'd mellowed in the intervening years. Max Slade would never mellow. In many ways, he was harder, more uncompromising, not as driven, not as optimistic. He had sacrificed his dream of a life in New York for the sake of the brothers who needed him and had no one else. The harsh realities of his life on a sprawling Wyoming ranch and his responsibility as guardian to three young boys had given him a depth he hadn't had four years ago.

To her distress, Calley found herself wanting to explore this complex man. Max was compelling, interesting, and she liked his company. She liked *him*.

She just wasn't so naive as to think she could ever be friends with him. There was, after all, that physical attraction, not to mention her impending departure.

"Would Jimmy be doing this if he were here?" she said.

"No. I'd just turn on the faucet and stick my arm under it."

"You tough cowboys."

He shrugged. "Works."

"Is that what you do when one of the boys gets hurt? Just stick the wounded body part under the faucet?"

"Depends."

"On what?"

"On how loud they're screaming."

She eyed him. "You're being sarcastic."

"Calley, I would never deliberately hurt one of those boys."

"I know. But you're an example to them. They watch everything you do, and they learn from it. If you stick your bloody arm under the faucet, they're going to think that's what they should do. Max—" She inhaled, the proximity of his bare chest in no way helping her powers of concentration. "Max, they deserve to see you happy."

He furrowed his brow. "What?"

"You know what I mean. They lured me out here not so we could be together, but so you could be happy. They didn't know me from a hole in the wall. But they know you. They want you to be happy. When I head to New York—" She hesitated, not sure she wasn't stepping into something she didn't want to be stepping in, something that was plainly none of her business. "I think you should try to have a romantic life after I've left."

"Who says I didn't have one before you got here?"

"Christopher and Timothy have said as much. So has Jimmy. Wynne, too, if not in as many words."

"Lucky been squealing, too?"

She grinned at him. "I haven't learned to talk turkey yet."

"Ha."

"Max, don't make this any more difficult than it is. You know damned well what I'm trying to tell you."

"Suppose I've been having a romantic life while you're here?"

"That's not funny."

He seemed to smile and grimace at the same time. "Who says I'm trying to be funny?"

She ignored him. He was amusing himself at her expense, probably trying to keep his mind occupied on something besides his injury, maybe even besides their physical closeness. "I should bandage this thing. It'll need gauze and tape to hold the wound closed, but I don't think it needs stitches."

"Jimmy keeps the first-aid kit on top of the refrigerator."

While she got it down, Max moved to the kitchen table, seemingly oblivious to his wound. He sat still, staring out at the raw, beautiful landscape that belonged to him and his brothers. In the past two weeks, Calley had never sensed that he'd regretted his decision to return home after his father's and Lissa Slade's deaths. It had meant losing her, but he'd made his peace with that loss.

In her own way, maybe so had she.

So why didn't she feel at peace?

She set the first-aid kit down on the table and opened it up. With no ambulance readily available to Black Creek Ranch at a moment's notice, it was fair sized and well stocked. After a few seconds' rummaging around, she found antibiotic ointment, a ball of gauze, adhesive tape and ancient scissors.

Max looked up at her. ''Never figured you for a nurse, Calley.''

''We New Yorkers are a resourceful bunch.''

''You always were one to rise to the occasion.''

She gave him an irreverent grin. ''So were you.'' Before he could reply, she snipped off a length of gauze. ''Now, hold out your arm, and let me know if I'm pulling too tight. I wouldn't want to make things worse.''

The bleeding had subsided, but Calley was careful as she dabbed on a little of the antibiotic ointment and wound the gauze around his rock-hard upper arm, securing it as best she could with the adhesive tape. She had to hack off a couple of lengths before she got one that didn't curl back up on itself, proof she was no nurse. Max remained patient, watching her in silence, no evidence he was in any pain. She could feel his slate eyes on her as she worked. They seemed softer than they had that first night at the airport. Or maybe that was what she wanted to see, hoped to see. A softer Max Slade. A Max Slade who was less remote, less hard to read.

What she ought to see, she thought, was what was there. The real Max Slade. Not the one of memory, not the one of hope.

His arm bandaged, he got to his feet. ''Thanks.''

She nodded. ''It'll probably throb awhile. Watch out for nails next time.''

"I guess I should be glad it was only a nail I ran into, the mood I was in." He headed back to the sink, scooping his shirt up off the floor. "Jimmy's out for the night, too, you know."

"He told me he has to get off the ranch once a year or he goes nuts."

Max grinned. "You believe him?"

"I smell a conspiracy."

"So do I." He slung his shirt over one shoulder, and she couldn't help but notice the movement of muscles in his shoulders and chest. "The Parkers offer to take all three boys for the night, and Jimmy suddenly needs to visit his daughter up in Cody."

"Daughter? I didn't hear that part."

"He was married once, aeons ago. Had a daughter. She's as stubborn and miserable as he is. Jimmy likes to see her when he can. Sometimes she comes down here. They can usually stand each other about twenty-four hours."

Calley laughed. "Jimmy does defy stereotyping."

"Most people do. Well, conspiracy or not, it's going to be a quiet night. I plan to stay up for a while, wait until this thing stops throbbing." He glanced at her as he started out of the kitchen, his taciturn mood seeming to subside. "You?"

She shrugged, suddenly aware of how quiet the place was without Jimmy grumbling and the boys racing around. "I guess I'll turn in early and read. Hope your arm feels better. If you need me for anything—" She swallowed, unable to imagine Max Slade needing anyone for anything. Or admitting to it if he did. "You know where to find me."

"For the next two days, anyway."

After an hour alone in her room reading a lurid horror novel, Calley would have welcomed the ungodly screech of the barn owl to break the silence. The rain had stopped. The dogs and turkey and other critters had settled down for the night. There was no wind. Of course, there were no cars, horns, taxis, sirens—none of the sounds she'd come to regard as background noise in New York and as a part of her life. Just silence. And darkness.

And thoughts of Max Slade in the living room, her only company for miles.

She turned a page in her book. Really, she could have picked something more conducive to calm and relaxation.

A knock on her door sent the book flying, but she swallowed a scream just in time.

"Calley?" Max called through the door. "Are you awake?"

"Yes, I'm awake," she said irritably. "It's too damned quiet around here to sleep. Something wrong?"

"I need a hand."

A hand. Great. As if *she* needed another distraction. She sighed, throwing off her quilted covers. "I'll be right there—"

"No, don't get up. If you're decent, I can just come in. I'll only be a minute."

She was in her Mets nightshirt. She was *in bed,* for heaven's sake. By definition, she wasn't decent, not to entertain Max Slade, injured or not. But if she went out to him, she would still be in her nightshirt, which came just to midthigh, and it was a chilly evening, the fabric of her nightshirt thin.

Maybe it was best he come in to her.

"Okay," she said without enthusiasm.

The door opened. Max walked in wearing nothing but jeans. He dropped a roll of gauze and adhesive tape and a pair of scissors onto the edge of the bed. Nothing in his demeanor suggested he even noticed she was sitting up in bed in her Mets nightshirt. The man had ripped open his arm on a nail, she reminded herself. He probably wasn't up to noticing her or anything else. Just because she noticed everything about him didn't mean he was as prone to such insanity.

"I need you to change my bandage," he said, his voice clipped, his expression grim. His eyes fell on her. She felt her mouth go dry at their intensity, no matter what they saw or didn't see. "If you don't mind."

Blood had oozed through the current bandage, which also had loosened considerably, probably because it was the creation of an amateur. Given the logistics, it would be difficult for him to rebandage the wound himself.

Calley met his probing gaze. "Not just going to stick your arm under the faucet?"

He managed a curt smile. "Not with Florence Nightingale in the house."

"You shouldn't be sarcastic with someone who can inflict pain on you. All right, I'll do the best I can. No point in having you get lockjaw on me."

"I said my tetanus shots are up-to-date—"

She eyed him. "Don't push me, Max. It won't take much to get me to change my mind and make you wrap a towel around that arm and be satisfied with it."

He laughed, offering no evidence he was in any pain whatsoever. "Infection, then. No point in having my arm get infected on you."

"There. I knew a good rationalization was lurking somewhere. Here, sit down."

She scooted over, making room for him. She silently thanked whatever force in her life was responsible for her dislike of slinky nightgowns. She was conscious enough of her state of dress as it was.

Max, she recalled, had never been a Mets fan.

"I'll cut off the old bandage first," she said, keeping her tone perfunctory and her mind on the matter at hand. She grabbed up the scissors and unceremoniously stuck one blade under the bandage and snipped it in two.

Max watched her dubiously. "I can see why you mind other people's money. Your bedside manner leaves a lot to be desired."

"I didn't cut you, did I?"

"You could have checked to make sure the bandage wasn't stuck to the wound."

"Was it?"

"No."

She grinned. "Lucky for you, huh?"

"I'd say it was lucky for you."

She dropped the bloody bandage onto the floor, to be disposed of later. "Your threats don't scare me, Max Slade. In any pain?"

"Not at the moment."

"That's what I figured. Looks as if the bleeding's stopped again. Want any antibiotic ointment?"

He shook his head, his slate eyes narrowed on her as she continued, rather inefficiently, with her work. Her hands were shaking. This time, it wasn't because of nervousness. It was, quite simply, because Max Slade was on her bed.

But not *in* it. There was a difference, she reminded herself.

"Hold still," she ordered. "Let me get a good look at this thing before I cover it up again." She peered at the jagged wound, but saw nothing that struck her as out of the ordinary, except for the well-developed muscle. "Did you hit your arm on something and open it up?"

"Must have. I don't really remember. I've been distracted today."

"A lot on your mind?"

"Mmm." His eyes stayed on her, darkening.

"I guess the ranch is a big responsibility." She kept her tone light as she tended his wound, her mouth still dry, awareness—of him, of herself, of the dark, quiet night—swirling through her. "There's more involved in raising and minding a bunch of horses than I ever thought."

"It's not the ranch," he said.

She swallowed. "Hold your arm out some so I can get the gauze around it."

Without comment, he did as she asked. She slipped the length of gauze under his arm, her fingers brushing against his chest. It had been distracting before, in the kitchen. Now, with nightfall and their intimate surroundings, it was downright unnerving. She lost her grip on the bandage, but caught it up again.

Max noticed. "Nervous?" he asked.

She licked her lips, aware of him watching her. "I just don't want to hurt you."

"You won't." His smile almost reached his eyes. "I'm tough."

"Not as tough as that nail you snagged." She had him hold the bandage in place while she cut a piece of adhesive tape, having less trouble with it folding back on itself than she had earlier. "If I ever live out in the wilderness, I'd make sure I took a class in advanced first aid. Of course, Jimmy says this really isn't the wilderness."

"By his standards, it's not."

"Well, he's never been to New York."

"True. That's more his idea of the wilderness."

In another few seconds, she had the bandage secured. "There," she said, proudly, her relief palpable as she sat back away from him. "Done."

"Thanks."

She looked at him. "I didn't hurt you, did I?"

"No. Calley—" He raised a hand, brushing his knuckles across her cheek. "You didn't hurt me."

"Max—"

"I was the one who hurt you. I wish I never had. I wish I could have that day back four years ago when I didn't finish my letter to you, didn't call, didn't come see you."

"Me, too. Not so you could have called me, but so I could have tracked you down. It wouldn't have been difficult. Look how fast your brothers found me. I could have found you. If you'd been the heel I thought you were, I could have had my revenge and gone on with my life." She twisted her hands together, wishing they would stop trembling. "But what's done is done."

"I'm glad you came to Wyoming, Calley."

She nodded. "Me, too." Awareness and arousal shimmered through her, startlingly powerful, impossible to ignore. "My friends are all tired of hearing me curse you to the rafters."

He smiled, touching one finger to the corner of her mouth. This time, she was telling him the truth, admitting in her own way she'd been hurt. "You must have missed me to keep cursing me after four years."

"You're such a cocky bastard, Slade."

His smile broadened, and he leaned in closer, his mouth almost on hers. "Tell me you didn't miss me."

Arousal washed through her, sensitizing every inch of her body. She could have kicked him out. He would have gone. She trusted him to leave if she asked him to.

But she didn't want to ask him to leave.

And there it was, she thought. The undeniable, simple truth of the matter. She wanted Max to stay with her, to make love to her. There was no doubt in her mind.

"Did *you* miss *me*?" she asked softly.

His hand dropped from her face, down her neck, then skimmed her breasts. She gasped at the sensations pulsing through her. His eyes locked with hers. "Every day," he whispered, and his mouth closed over hers. He explored, tasted, teased until her breath came in short, shallow gasps. They fell back together against the pillows. Somehow, he caught the hem of her nightshirt and raised it up, gazing all the while at the skin he exposed, as if drinking in the very sight of her. She'd never experienced anything so erotic.

"I've dreamed about this moment," he murmured, sliding both hands, his wound not interfering, up her abdomen, until he cupped her breasts with his palms. His mouth followed. She could feel herself losing control. Then he slipped one hand between her thighs, and she cried out.

He raised his eyes to her. "Did you miss me, Calley?"

"Yes. I tried to make myself stop, but I couldn't."

"I know. There were times I thought I'd die if I didn't see you."

She shut her eyes at his admission and tried to tell herself he was just speaking out of the passion of the moment, that she couldn't take his words to heart. But she found that she wanted to believe him. Needed to.

He pulled the nightshirt over her head, and she opened her eyes as he cast it aside, gazing at her as if for the first time. To her surprise, she felt no embarrassment, no awkwardness, just the overwhelming sensation that this was right. He was different. She was different. Yet what they'd been together four years ago was a part of them.

"Calley..."

"It's okay. I'm not changing my mind."

His eyes reached hers, but he said nothing, swiftly removing his jeans and discarding them in a heap. When he came back to her, his body was sleek and hard and even sexier than she remembered. She wanted to touch him, feel him, stroke him everywhere. She would never get enough of him, she realized. She would never stop wanting him. It wasn't just physical desire at work; it was the longings of her heart, her very soul.

But he had broken her heart. Four years later, she finally knew why. Four years later, she finally understood. There was, however, no going back and picking up where they'd left off. If loving Max Slade was a part of her, so was being angry with him, knowing how deeply he'd hurt her, then accepting it and moving on.

All she could do was open herself to him, to herself and her own need and longings. She wanted to feel him pulsing inside her again. She wanted to ease the unspeakable ache that had her quivering and quaking all over.

"Max...there's something...I need to tell you...." She caught her breath, willed herself to be coherent. "There's been no one else since you."

He got her meaning immediately, inhaled deeply, his control shredded. "Calley..."

"Don't. Don't say anything else. It doesn't affect anything. I just wanted you to know."

"But you sacrificed—"

"I didn't sacrifice a thing, Max." She ran one palm up his smooth, hard back and smiled to herself. "Not a thing. New York's social life isn't all it's cracked up to be, I guess."

"I never would have expected you not to have anyone else."

She gave him a wry smile. "I didn't expect it of myself."

"It wouldn't have mattered—"

"It *doesn't* matter."

He kissed her then, a long, deep kiss that made her glad she'd spoken up when she had, because now she couldn't speak, couldn't even begin to articulate any of what she thought or felt with any coherency. She couldn't remember wanting him as much as she did now. In every way she could manage, she communicated that want to him, until finally, slick and hard with need himself, he slipped inside her, and all she'd felt for him four long, long years ago was fresh again.

Later, when the night was again quiet and they lay together in the darkness, she could feel him breathing, and she knew she never wanted to be without him in her life.

But out of nowhere, he said, "I mean to keep my promise to you."

"What promise?"

He turned onto his side, his eyes lost in the dark night. "To put you on your plane back to New York."

"Then tonight doesn't matter?"

"It matters. It just doesn't change anything. You belong in New York," he said, "and I belong here."

Long after Max had fallen asleep, Calley lay with her eyes wide open. Max Slade was a stubborn man, determined to do the right thing by her, especially after their last, disastrous parting. And she'd forced him to make that blasted promise. He *would* put her on a plane to New York. In his mind, it would be the right thing to do.

Well, she thought, snuggling closer to him, she would just have to outwit him. As she drifted off to sleep, a plan started to form.

# 10

Saying goodbye to Timothy and Wynne was painful, but saying goodbye to Christopher was worst of all. Calley found him out back behind the stable waiting for Fred to slither out of his hole.

"I think I'm going to write a poem about snakes," he said without looking up at her.

"What kind of snakes?"

"All kinds."

"You've seen your share, I suppose."

He squinted up at her, too much knowledge, too much disappointment, in those young Slade eyes. "I have."

It wasn't even nine o'clock, a bright, sunny, startlingly clear morning. Calley had on a functional travel outfit of black chinos, white shirt and sneakers. Max was insisting on driving her to the airport. She hadn't bothered trying to argue him out of making her go back to New York. She had extracted a promise from him to make her go. He needed to keep that promise. She needed him to keep it.

But she didn't want to go.

She cleared her throat, reminding herself that Christopher Slade had endured far worse pain than having a woman he'd known for all of two weeks head back home. But there had been all those weeks on the computer, too. "You still have my E-mail address. You can write to me."

He shrugged his bony shoulders. "I might."

"Christopher—"

"You'd better go. You don't want to miss your plane."

"Christopher, I want you to know I don't regret coming to Wyoming. I've had a wonderful time. I'm not sorry you weren't Jill Baxter." She smiled, but he'd turned back to his snake hole. She sighed. "I'm glad you're you."

He ignored her.

It had been a lame statement anyway. She was glad he was Christopher Slade instead of Jill Baxter. At least the kid had known all along who *he* was. The problem was who Calley was. Who she was, what she wanted, where she wanted to be. When she'd come to Wyoming, she thought she knew. She was Calley Hastings of New York, New York, financial planner, a woman who loathed Max Slade.

Well, she was still a financial planner, still Calley Hastings.

"I've got to go," she said, her voice cracking. Not since she'd been a kid herself had a kid seen her cry. What good would tears do Christopher Slade?

He didn't look back at her. "So go ahead. Go."

She touched his shoulder. He had on a ragged T-shirt, ragged shorts. He had plenty of nonragged clothes. She figured it was his penniless-poet look. He was eleven, after all. Still trying on new identities. In a way, so was she.

"Christopher, if you'll promise..."

But she stopped herself. She couldn't make him promise not to tell Max something. Max was his older brother, his guardian and as much as he would ever have in the way of a father. It would be irresponsible to undermine their trust in each other. She bit down on one corner of her mouth. Such complications. Of course, she'd never been one to think parenting would be easy.

Christopher turned to her, expectant.

She sighed. "There's no reason we can't still be friends."

He looked back at his snake hole, disgusted.

There was no patronizing the kid, Calley thought. He saw through everything. She inhaled, hating to see him so obviously disappointed that her two weeks on Black Creek Ranch had come to naught. But her relationship with his big brother was complicated, and there were things about her and Max an eleven-year-old just didn't need to know.

"Okay. I'll be as straight with you as I can."

He refused to meet her eyes one more time. Jimmy would have climbed all over him for being rude, but Calley understood. Somewhere, deep in that cowboy poet's soul of his, Christopher Slade knew that she and Max were in love with each other.

"Just remember," she said to his back. "I have a plan."

He shot her a quick, sideways look, then gave her a grin that was pure, conniving, unadulterated Slade.

Max, his three younger brothers and Jimmy Baxter arrived in New York on a warm, clear summer day ten days after Max had put Calley Hastings on her plane east. She hadn't kicked and screamed. She hadn't begged to stay in Wyoming. She had simply said, "I'm glad I came, Max. I enjoyed meeting your brothers and Jimmy and seeing the ranch. It was a good vacation. I guess I needed the break more than I realized. New York will probably never be the same to me again."

She had intended, Max was quite certain, to sound as if she were being perfectly sensible and meant to get on with her life and stay in New York where she belonged. She wouldn't kick and scream and pitch a fit and pretend she wanted to live with him and Jimmy and his three brothers on a ranch in Wyoming.

But Max had detected a gleam in her eye, a kick in her step, that suggested Calley Hastings was devising herself a big plot.

In the past, her plots had usually involved money. Now that she'd seen Wyoming, Max just didn't know. He'd let her go, expecting he would find out his answer soon enough.

Then, a day or two after her departure, Jimmy had let it slip about the carpenters.

"What carpenters?" Max had said.

"Uh—uh—" Jimmy had said.

"Jimmy, what's going on?"

"Calley—well—she—" But Jimmy was no good at dissembling, and he'd finally spit it out in his own way. "That woman of yours wants to turn my storage room into an office. She lined up carpenters to come take a look."

"Whose office?"

"Nope. Uh-uh. I said I'd keep my mouth shut."

Then, after that, the delivery man had arrived with the mountain bikes and the tent.

"What mountain bikes?" Max had asked. "What tent?"

Christopher had bit back a grin as if he knew exactly what mountain bikes, what tent. He and his two younger brothers tore open the boxes. Wynne produced a card and immediately recognized Calley's name on it, jumping up and down with unseemly delight. Timothy had grabbed the card out of his hand and read it. "Calley—um—she says this is a thank-you present."

"A thank-you for what?" Max had growled.

"For her vacation. 'If it weren't for you boys, I might never have seen Wyoming. I hope you like my surprise.'"

It had been one hell of a surprise. With five mountain bikes and a tent big enough for a platoon on his front porch, Max knew what the gleam in Calley's eye had been all about. A graceful exit from Black Creek Ranch just wasn't in her.

"I think she's coming back," Wynne had blurted.

Christopher couldn't stop grinning. The rascal *knew* she was coming back. Max just couldn't be sure if it was that damned poet's soul of his talking, or if Calley had taken him into her confidence. He wasn't going to put the kid on the spot by demanding to know which it was.

Instead, he'd booked five round-trip tickets to New York, New York.

He was relieved the weather wasn't hazy, hot and humid. The boys might not have minded, but sweltering heat would have sent Jimmy right back to Wyoming. It was all the old cowboy could do to endure traffic, noise, tall buildings and millions of people crammed together. He had only agreed to come because Max needed him to watch the boys while he got to the bottom of Calley Hastings—and her carpenters, tents and mountain bikes.

They took a cab to their small, boutique-style hotel on the Upper East Side. It was built at the turn of the century, located in the midst of some of New York's finest museums, which thrilled Christopher. Timothy was more intrigued by the bagelry down on the corner. He couldn't wait to try New York bagels. Wynne was happy just riding the ornate elevator. Jimmy tolerated his surroundings as he would a desert dust storm. He muttered incessantly about smog, claustrophobia and the hotel's decor, which apparently reminded him of a "house of ill repute" he'd "heard of" back in his old cowboy days.

Max had promised the boys a ball game and visits to the Empire State Building, the Statue of Liberty and the dinosaur skeletons in the Museum of Natural History.

They just had to give him time to deal with Calley.

"You don't know where she lives?" Timothy asked.

"Oh, I know where she lives. She hates to move. She has an apartment on the Upper West Side, across Central Park from us. We're on the Upper East Side."

"East side of what?" Christopher asked.

"Manhattan's an island. The numbered streets go across it, east to west. The further north, the higher the number. The avenues run lengthwise, north to south. Fifth Avenue's the dividing line between east and west. Check out your map. There's a logic to it."

"Wow," Wynne said, as if he understood everything Max had said.

Christopher was gazing out one of the windows in the suite Max had reserved. "I can't believe you used to live here."

"For seven years," Max said, trying to remember the man he'd been then. Seven years in New York, four years in Wyoming. A lot had changed.

Wynne emerged from the bathroom with a little basket of complimentary toiletries, which he promptly dumped on the bed. Max smiled. His brothers would have a grand time during their week in New York. It wouldn't take much to keep them happy. An elevator, a view of the street, little bars of soap.

Jimmy was another matter. He was pacing back and forth with his bad leg, muttering about city folk.

"The hotel offers a complimentary afternoon tea," Max told him. "Maybe you can take the boys down while I'm gone. They have a live harpist."

Jimmy grunted. "Better'n a dead one."

Max laughed, and headed out into the streets of Manhattan. He knew he didn't belong here, not anymore. There was no question of that. The only question, he thought, was where Calley Hastings thought she belonged.

Calley walked up West End Avenue, barely aware of the crush of rush-hour traffic as she enjoyed the beautiful late-summer afternoon. No matter what her future held, she knew she would always love New York. It was her city. It was where she had established her career and made so many friends, and it was where she had first fallen in love with Max Slade.

She had fallen in love with him a second time on Black Creek Ranch, Wyoming.

Of all places, she thought. Who would have ever guessed it? She glanced up at the residential buildings of the Upper West Side. In many ways, Wyoming might have been on another planet. Yet she could almost smell the wildflowers in the meadow beyond the stables, hear the horses in the pasture. Her friends thought she was coming unglued. Why *Wyoming?* they would say. Because Max Slade was there. Ah, they would counter, wasn't he the one who'd turned her off romance? Hadn't she found a dried rose he'd given her for Valentine's Day and burned it and thrown the ashes off her roof?

Yes. That was her Max. He was pig-headed and stupidly honorable and utterly reliable, if only he could trust her to make up her own mind about things.

By the time she reached the lobby of her building, she'd worked up a good head of steam.

And there was Max Slade, chatting with the doorman. He might have just climbed off a horse. Nothing about him suggested he'd ever lived in New York or ever would.

Calley stood rock still. Maybe she'd just conjured him up. After a week, she was allowed.

Then his slate eyes fell on her. He was real.

She inhaled. "Max."

"Afternoon, Calley."

"What are you doing here?"

"Rumor has it someone in this building's been fantasizing about a tall, dark rancher sweeping her off to Wyoming."

She felt blood rush to her cheeks as the doorman looked at her in surprised amusement. She cleared her throat. Max Slade certainly could play havoc with her reputation. "You're not supposed to be here—"

He smiled, confident. "I know."

"You—" She frowned, growing wary. "What do you know?"

"Maybe we should talk up in your apartment."

She glanced at the doorman, who was watching with interest, never having seen Calley Hastings with a man so obviously not from the East. She didn't remember Max sticking out four years ago. But, of course, that was one of the reasons he'd gone back to Wyoming.

Because deep down, he'd known he was trying to be something he wasn't in New York, trying to fit into a life in which he didn't belong. She understood that now.

But first she had to get him out of her lobby.

"I'm on the tenth floor," she said, briskly leading the way to the elevator.

"I remember."

His voice, deep and deliberately languid, curled up her spine. She banged the Up button. Fortunately, the elevator was right there. Unfortunately, it was small and without air-conditioning. Standing next to him, she found herself assaulted with memories of the second time they'd made love that night in Wyoming, their bodies hot and wanting.

He smiled. "You're squirming, Calley."

"I can't believe you're here."

"The element of surprise," he said.

"Are you alone?"

"Jimmy's with the boys back at the hotel."

New Yorker that she was, she couldn't resist asking him which hotel. His choice met her approval, especially if he planned to take the boys to the major museums. She started to suggest restaurants, but Max stopped her.

"Calley, I'm not here just to show the boys around New York."

She licked her lips. "Max—I'm not—I can't—" She sighed. "Dammit, I'm not *ready* for you."

He leaned back against the elevator, one leg bent. Cocky, sexy. Amused. "You never will be."

That brought her up straight. "You're such a smug bastard, Slade."

"And you're so much fun to catch in the act. Spoiled your plans, didn't I?"

She tossed her head back. "Maybe not. Maybe it's better this way."

The elevator stopped, and the doors opened. Calley went ahead of him. She could feel his presence close behind her. He made no smart remarks about life in New York as she unlocked the series of locks on her door and pushed it open.

"After you," she said, motioning broadly.

Her one-bedroom apartment was small and charming, bathed in the strong late-afternoon sunlight. In the four years since Max had exited from her life, she'd added personal touches, making the place feminine, sophisticated, very much a reflection of her own personality. She'd painted the walls in shades of cranberry, had the love seat and high-backed chair covered in a flowered print, put up chintz drapes, as if thumbing her nose at the idea of ever sharing her space with a man.

Max seemed as out of place standing in front of her butler's table in her living room as she must have seemed caught in a staring match with his Frisbee-playing turkey out on Black Creek Ranch. Yet he didn't seem to mind. He didn't seem any less masculine, any less confident of himself and his mission.

"Something to drink?" Calley asked briskly.

"Ice tea would be nice."

On Black Creek Ranch, Jimmy Baxter would put out a huge jar and make "sun tea." Calley used a mix, sometimes cans. When the mood struck and she had the time, she would make up a pot of loose-leaf tea and pour it over ice. But she offered no apologies when she returned to the living room with two tall glasses of ice tea from a mix. She'd made sure there was no powder on the edge of Max's glass. Hers she didn't care about. She was so taken aback by his presence she could have been drinking straight powder.

Max sipped his ice tea without comment. Calley followed his gaze to the fabric swatches spread out on the butler's table and the stack of wallpaper books underneath it. She winced. Caught in the act indeed.

"Redoing your apartment?" he asked. His tone was deceptively mild. He was daring her to lie to him.

He knew everything, Calley decided. She took a huge gulp of her ice tea. "Jimmy ratted me out?"

"You ratted yourself out. You went behind my back. You tried to manipulate me."

"Manipulate *you?*" she scoffed. "That I'd like to see."

"You know what you did."

She shrugged, drinking more of her tea, trying to ignore the shaking in her knees. "A tactical decision."

"Calley."

"That's the truth."

"You made me look like a bad guy to my whole family."

"How?"

"One, it seems I don't know what's going on in my own house. Carpenters, tents, mountain bikes. Two—"

"You forgot the air mattresses," Calley said, dropping onto the love seat before her knees gave out. This wasn't going according to plan. Max had messed up everything.

He glared at her. He wasn't about to sit down. "What air mattresses?"

"They must be on back order. Well, that surprise is out of the bag."

"Calley."

She blinked at him. "You don't think I'd go camping without an air mattress, do you?"

"Who said anything about you going camping?"

"Yes. Well. Never mind about that, then. Go on. What's the second way I made you look like a villain?"

He bit off a sigh. He wasn't finished with her camping plans, she could see. "All right. I'll move on. My family thinks I'm the villain because I'm the one who put you on the plane back to New York."

"You didn't force me onto the plane at gunpoint."

"But I didn't ask you to stay."

She waved a hand in dismissal. "It wouldn't have made any difference. You were honor bound to make sure I got back home, even if I'd said I wanted to stay."

"Which you didn't," he argued.

"True."

He moved toward her, his expression unreadable. "Calley, what are you trying to accomplish?"

She leaned back and crossed her legs, swinging her ankle, trying to look more casual than she felt. "I am trying to get you to let me decide for myself what I want and where I belong. I am trying to get you to *trust* me."

"Let you?" He tightened both hands into fists as he obviously reined in his self-control. "I'd like to know who the hell could keep you from doing something you set your mind to."

"You did four years ago when you left New York. You didn't give me the chance to make up my own mind about what I wanted." She spoke quietly, without anger, because she felt none. She'd come a long way in her opinion of Max Slade since departing for Wyoming several weeks ago. "I understand why you did what you did. But I'm not going to allow your sense of duty and honor to determine my course of action. I had to find a way to convince you that I—to show you that I—" She broke off, floundering, annoyed with herself.

"That you what, Calley?"

His eyes, his voice, his stance—everything about Max was intense, on alert. She shifted restlessly on the love seat, then exhaled at the ceiling. "That I deserve to make up my own mind."

"Ah." His tone was disbelieving, as if he knew she would back away from telling him the whole truth. "Am I to conclude by your conduct you want to move to Wyoming?"

"That would be one conclusion."

"What would be another?"

"I want to go camping."

He gave her a hard, dark look. "Calley."

She shot to her feet, agitated, suddenly very warm. "Max, maybe you did me a favor four years ago. You made it easy for me to stay here. If you'd asked me to go with you to Wyoming with your father and Lissa dead and three confused, grieving little boys to raise, I don't know what I would have done. I might have gone with you, I might have stayed in New York. It doesn't matter. It's a moot point. But I've had four additional years here. I've had a great life." She gave him a small smile. "Even loathing you became sort of fun. My combat wounds, so to speak."

He didn't smile back. "I wish I could have found a way not to hurt you."

"No. No, don't, Max. Don't beat yourself up over what you did. You tried to spare me. You tried to do the right thing by your brothers, your father, the people who make their living off the ranch. You *did* do the right thing. And that's not my point. Yes, I love New York. It has its problems, but I love its energy, the people, my work."

"I wouldn't ask you to give up your life here."

She held up a hand, stopping him, trying not to relent before she'd finished. "But I fell for a sob story about a widow in Wyoming not just because Christopher, Timothy and Wynne were good, but because I was a prime candidate for swallowing such a story.

Something was missing in my own life. I think I went to Wyoming to see if I could figure out what it was.''

"Did you?" Max asked softly, not moving toward her.

"Yes. It was missing you, the boys, Jimmy, the ranch.''

"Calley—"

"The carpenters, the tent, the mountain bikes, the air mattresses—they were just an attempt to find a way to get you to believe that I've changed. I'm not the same woman who needed to stay in New York four years ago.''

"Calley." His voice was more insistent, and she stopped, giving him his chance to speak. He moved close to her, then ran his thumb along her lower lip. Just that feathery touch sent shivers of awareness through her. Finally, he said, "Tell me where you belong.''

"You won't believe me.''

"Tell me, Calley.''

She swallowed, meeting his dark eyes. "I belong with you.''

For a long moment, he didn't speak, and neither did she. Then he withdrew something from the pocket of his tan canvas pants and handed it to her.

It was a ticket from Jackson, Wyoming, to New York, New York. Calley glanced at it, confused. He was here. Obviously, he'd flown.

"Look at the purchase date," he said.

She did so. The ticket had been purchased the same

day she'd left Wyoming for New York over a week ago. She frowned at him. "I don't understand."

He smiled. "I bought this ticket the minute you took off. I knew I had to find a way to keep you in my life. If it came to it, I was willing to divide my time between New York and Wyoming, anything if it meant not losing you. Then Jimmy spilled the news about your devious ways, then that stuff landed on my porch and I figured I had to fight fire with fire. So here we are."

"Max—"

"I love you, Calley Hastings. I have for a long, long time." He kissed her deeply, gently, and whispered into her mouth, "And I believe you."

# *Epilogue*

—➤◆◀—

Christopher tacked up pictures of Max and Calley's wedding on the bulletin board in his room, next to the pictures of his trip to New York City. They'd gotten married right away in a simple service held at the ranch. They figured they'd waited long enough. Jimmy and John Parker had cooked, and friends from New York and Wyoming had come. Even Max's mother had flown in from San Francisco. Wynne had served as ring bearer. Timothy as usher. Christopher had served as his brother's best man.

There was one picture of the five of them, with the dogs lying at their feet and Lucky holding in his beak the new, shocking pink Frisbee Calley had bought him. Max had vetoed Timothy fetching Fred.

But Christopher's eyes kept drifting to his pictures of New York. What a trip. He would never forget it. He'd particularly loved the Statue of Liberty and the view of the New York skyline at night. He'd told Max he wanted to live in New York someday. Max had said that would be fine, if it was what Christopher wanted. He knew their father hadn't been so agreeable when

Max had expressed the same desire. But Christopher also knew that Max would never hold his brothers to the ranch.

Timothy was downstairs playing the piano. Calley had had it tuned. She played in the evening sometimes. Christopher tolerated ragtime, but he wasn't much on most of the other stuff she played.

Wynne was "helping" Calley and Max wallpaper her new office. The carpenters had left yesterday, after expanding Jimmy's old storage room to her liking. She had lots of windows with views of the mountains and the river. Her equipment would be arriving in a few days. She already had a half-dozen clients.

His last wedding picture tacked up, Christopher grabbed his blank book and ventured downstairs. He had no desire to be put to work. He particularly hated wallpapering. He slipped past Timothy at the piano out to the front porch, then ran around back to the stable. It was a coolish, late-summer evening, perfect for his purposes.

He ducked into the storage room and pulled on the light bulb overhead. Max's old trunk was gone. Calley had appropriated it for her office, and they'd all gone through the photo albums together, her and Max and Timothy and Wynne and Christopher. Even Jimmy had checked out a few of the pictures, commenting on how full of himself Max was back in those days. Christopher had snuck out the one of his brother and Calley on the steps of what he now knew was the New York Metropolitan Museum of Fine Arts. He'd had it blown up and framed for their wedding present.

But now he sat on the floor of the storage room and leaned back against the old desk, and opened his blank book. He closed his eyes and thought of his mother and his father, and then of Max just that morning at breakfast, smiling the way he had in that picture on the museum steps four years ago. And he thought of a poem, and he wrote.

\* \* \* \* \*

*Sneak Previews of July titles,
from Yours Truly™*

## THE CASE OF THE LADY IN APARTMENT 308
### by Lass Small

*Ed Hollingsworth's observations about the lady in apartment 308:* great figure, nice smile (when she does smile), strange friends, kooky habits. His first thought had been *eviction,* but now Ed's hoping to take his investigation directly behind sexy Marcia Phillips's closed door....

## WHEN MAC MET HAILEY
### by Celeste Hamilton

*Hailey on Mac:* He's cute, a great kisser...but a single dad! I've already been down that road before....
*Mac on Hailey:* My friends think I should date someone nice, maybe find a mom for my young daughter. The one hot number I keep coming back to is Hailey's....

# Take 4 bestselling love stories FREE

## Plus get a FREE surprise gift!

# This July, watch for the delivery of...

An exciting new miniseries that appears in a different Silhouette series each month. It's about love, marriage—and Daddy's unexpected need for a baby carriage!

Daddy Knows Last unites five of your favorite authors as they weave five connected stories about baby fever in New Hope, Texas.

- **THE BABY NOTION** by Dixie Browning (SD#1011, 7/96)

- **BABY IN A BASKET** by Helen R. Myers (SR#1169, 8/96)

- **MARRIED...WITH TWINS!** by Jennifer Mikels (SSE#1054, 9/96)

- **HOW TO HOOK A HUSBAND (AND A BABY)** by Carolyn Zane (YT#29, 10/96)

- **DISCOVERED: DADDY** by Marilyn Pappano (IM#746, 11/96)

Daddy Knows Last arrives in July...only from

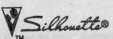

TM

DKLT

**SILHOUETTE®**

# *Desire*®
## CELEBRATION 1000

### is on its way
### in April, May and June 1996!

Join us for the celebration of Desire's 1000th book! We'll have

- Book #1000, *Man of Ice* by Diana Palmer in May!
- Best-loved miniseries such as **Hawk's Way** by Joan Johnston, and **Daughters of Texas** by Annette Broadrick
- Fabulous new writers in our Debut author program, where you can collect <u>**double**</u> Pages and Privileges Proofs of Purchase

Plus you can enter our exciting Sweepstakes for a chance to win a beautiful piece of original Silhouette Desire cover art or one of many autographed Silhouette Desire books!

**SILHOUETTE DESIRE'S CELEBRATION 1000**
...because the best is yet to come!

**The wedding celebration was so nice...
too bad the bride wasn't there!**

*Runaway Brides*

Find out what happens when three brides have a change of heart.

Three complete stories by some of your favorite authors—all in one special collection!

**YESTERDAY ONCE MORE**
by Debbie Macomber

**FULL CIRCLE**
by Paula Detmer Riggs

**THAT'S WHAT FRIENDS ARE FOR**
by Annette Broadrick

Available this June wherever books are sold.

Look us up on-line at:http://www.romance.net

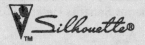

SREQ696

# You're About to Become a Privileged Woman

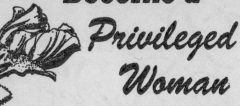

Reap the rewards of fabulous free gifts and benefits with proofs-of-purchase from Silhouette and Harlequin books

# Pages & Privileges™

It's our way of thanking you for buying our books at your favorite retail stores.

✂ PROOF OF PURCHASE
YT-PP145
Offer expires October 31, 1996

Harlequin and Silhouette—
the most privileged readers in the world!

For more information about Harlequin and Silhouette's PAGES & PRIVILEGES program call the Pages & Privileges Benefits Desk: 1-503-794-2499

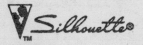

Silhouette®

YT-PP145